Sketches of
English Character

Sketches of English Character

Volume One

by Catherine Gore

NONSUCH

First published 1846
Copyright © in this edition 2005
Nonsuch Publishing Ltd

Nonsuch Publishing Limited
The Mill, Brimscombe Port, Stroud, Gloucestershire, GL5 2QG
www.nonsuch-publishing.com

British Library Cataloguing in Publication Data.
A catalogue record for this book is available from the British Library.

ISBN 1-84588-044-7

Typesetting and origination by Nonsuch Publishing Limited
Printed in Great Britain by Oaklands Book Services Limited

Contents

INTRODUCTION TO THE MODERN EDITION	7
INTRODUCTION	11
POPULAR PEOPLE	19
THE GOSSIP	27
SUSCEPTIBLE PEOPLE	35
PLAUSIBLE PEOPLE	43
THE CHAPERON AND THE DEBUTANTE	49
THE CABINET MINISTRESS	65
THE LINEMAN	73
THE STANDARD FOOTMAN	89
THE LADY'S-MAID	105
THE FAMILY BUTLER	115
THE FRENCH COOK	127
THE BODY-COACHMAN	139
THE BANKER	155
THE HOTEL-KEEPER	167
THE PRIVATE SECRETARY	177

Introduction to the Modern Edition

The best novel writer of her class and the wittiest woman of her age

The Times, 1861

SKETCHES OF ENGLISH CHARACTER, ONE of Catherine Gore's later works, was first published in 1846. She takes a selection of types of people, from a Lady's Maid to a Banker, and subjects them to satirical scrutiny. Some of those whom she sketches, such as the Chaperon and the Debutante and the Family Butler, no longer exist as she describes them, but if society has changed, human nature has not. Others, in particular the Gossip, are still with us in almost unaltered form.

Popular People, as Gore terms them, were the celebrities of their day: they were to be found everywhere, but nobody quite knew why. 'The greatest poets, preachers and senators,' as she reminds us, 'have however been the least popular.' The Gossip still finds plenty to say about the Popular People, and 'the English, taken as a mass, are decided gossips.' She has little time for Susceptible People, 'pigmies on stilts' who see insults everywhere, nor for Plausible People whose hypocrisy rings true today. The Chaperon and the Debutante, though nowadays more or less extinct, nonetheless illustrate how some people can become preoccupied with money or social status. The Cabinet Ministress, in contrast to the other examples of English character examined by Gore, is presented positively, and highlights the contribution made by spouses to official life, not only ministerial, but elsewhere, too.

Like the Chaperon and the Debutante, the Linkman, the Standard Footman, the Lady's Maid and the Family Butler have almost entirely disappeared from English society. The Royal Family and perhaps some of the aristocracy may still retain servants of one sort or another, but they are no longer as common as they were in 1846. She presents them in ascending order of their own perceived importance, which perhaps suggests the point which she is making: there were (and are) hierarchies in all parts of society. Once an errand-boy rises to the dignity of footman, he is no longer 'aware of the existence of the multitudinous untitled, saving as "the populace"', whereas the butler 'is a man so many degrees upraised above his origin, as to have cast aside his nature, and in every sense to have forgotten himself.' It is still the case that many regard the English as 'notoriously the most backward of civilized nations in the art of cookery', and the French Cook is held up as the master of that art. And, the Private Secretary, like his modern equivalent, the special advisor, continues to 'exercise considerable influence over the human nature and constitution.'

Shrewd and irreverent, Catherine Gore's sketches of stereotypical English characters provide perceptive insights into early Victorian society. Although written in the mid-nineteenth century, *Sketches of English Character* is a portrait of society that is still relevant at the beginning of the twenty-first.

Catherine Gore was born in 1799 in East Retford, Nottinghamshire, the daughter of Charles Moody, a wine merchant. Her literary talent asserted itself at an early age, and she wrote a concluding canto to Byron's 'Childe Harold' and a poem, 'The Graves of the North,' which, although unpublished, were praised by Joanna Baillie, the contemporary poet and playwright; her friends referred to her as 'the poetess.' It was not until after her marriage to Captain Charles Gore of the 1st Life Guards in 1823 that she published her first work, *The Broken Hearts*, a verse story. This was quickly followed, in 1824, by *Theresa Marchmont, or the Maid of Honour* and from then until 1849 she published a book almost every year, and in some years more than one.

As well as writing poems and novels, in 1827 Gore composed melodies for three works of Robert Burns, 'The Three Long Years,' 'Welcome, Welcome' and 'And ye shall walk in silk attire,' before turning her attention to play-writing. *The School for Coquettes* (1831) was produced at the Haymarket Theatre and ran for thirty nights; *Quid pro Quo, or the Days of Dupes* appeared in 1844, running for five weeks and winning the prize of £500 offered by Benjamin Webster for the best new original English comedy.

Gore is probably best remembered for her novels of the 'silver fork' genre, a term coined by William Hazlitt in 1827 to describe novels which recalled the elegance and fashion of the upper classes during the Regency. *Women As They Are, or the Manners of the Day* (1830) was praised by King George IV as 'the best bred and most amusing novel published in his remembrance'; *The Hamiltons, or the New Era* (1834) was lauded by such literary luminaries as William Thackeray and Charlotte Brontë. In all, she produced around seventy works and found great popularity with contemporary readers. She died at Linwood, Lyndhurst, Hampshire, in 1861.

Introduction

To pretend to characterize the classes or professions of a nation so late in the day as the middle of the nineteenth century, is a somewhat arduous task. In England, as elsewhere, every die is worn down,—every angle rounded,—every feature effaced,—every salient point smoothed, pummiced, and polished into the most level monotony of surface; a surface from which neither dramatist nor novelist can extract either plot or character, without violating in the grossest manner the probabilities of civilized life.

Singing is now far from the only feat that is accomplished "by the million." People eat, drink, sleep, talk, move, think in millions. No one *dares* to be himself, From Dan to Beersheba, not an original left! All the books published seem to have been copied from the same type, with one of Wedgewood's manifold. All the speeches made might be stereotyped in January by an able reporter, to last out till June. In society, men are packed one within the other, like forks or spoons in a plate chest, each of the same exact pattern and amount of pennyweights. Doctor, divine, or devil's-dragoman, (*Ang.* lawyer,) all dressed alike,—all affecting the same tastes, pursuits, and habits of life.

Would Shakspeare have invented Falstaff, or Parolles, in such an order of society? Would Scott have hit upon the Baron of Bradwardine, or Lawyer Pleydell? Would even Fielding or Smollett have extracted the ripe humour of their inventions out of such a sea of batter? The few authors of fiction who pretend to individualize, are obliged to have recourse to the most unsophisticated class for elements of character; society of a higher grade being so used down into tameness, as to form one long, long Baker Street, or Guildford Street, of mean, graceless, and tedious uniformity—from number one to number one hundred, a hundred times ditto repeated.

It is not so in other capitals. Elsewhere, every profession has its stamp, and every grade its distinctions. In Paris, or Berlin, or Vienna, you can no more surmise when you dine out what will be placed on the table, or what conversation will take place around it, than you can pre-assure the morrow's weather. In London, whether the dinner occur at the house of a man of eight hundred a year, or of eight thousand, you are cognizant, to a dish and a topic, what will be supplied for the delectation of your ears and palate. You eat the turbot and saddle of mutton by anticipation, as you go along; and may chew the cud of the great letters of the ministerial and opposition papers, which anon you will have to swallow, diluted with milk and water by the dull, or vivified by a few drops of alcohol by the brilliant.

In the evening entertainments, as at the dinners, "*toujours perdrix!*"—Jullien, Gunter, and Lord Flipflap,—Lord Flipflap, Gunter and Jullien!—You see the same people waltzing, fiddling, and serving the refreshments, and hear the same phrases exchanged among them, at every fete given at the west end of the town between May and August. May and August?—Rather say from A.D. 1835 to A.D. 1850!

This tedious uniformity of conventional life, which has converted society into a paper of pins with people stuck in rows, instead of minikins, is, we are told, the result of a high state of civilization. The moment the English left off clipping their yew-trees and laying down their gravel walks at right angles, they transferred the system to society. "Ye fallen avenues!" (so pathetically sung by Cowper,) you have now your parallels at every dinner party; and not a coterie in Grosvenor Square but presents the stiff unmeaning rectangularity of Hampton Court Gardens.

This eternal sameness of manners and opinions is, in fact, so notorious among ourselves, that no one ventures to say, "It is a fine day," till he have ascertained whether such be the opinion of Lord Rigmarole or Mr. Tompkins,—whosoever may be the Pope, or fugleman, or model man of his set. And yet England still retains on the continent the distinction of being "*le pays des originaux*;" and one of the first ejaculations of a foreigner to an English person with whom he is on confidential terms, is, "admit that you are the oddest people in the world!"

Useless were it to assert that, on the contrary, we are the evenest,—smooth as glass,—level as wood pavement; for, sooth to say, half the traits of English eccentricity cited by foreign journals are strictly true. Not a city on the continent but has witnessed some marvellous trait of English originality, some feat performed as for a wager;—for the moment an Englishman feels the pragmaticality of his native land too much for his spirits, off he goes, to relieve himself abroad; and, like a high-pressure boiler, of which the safety-valve has been obstructed, the explosion is terrible.

A man of peculiar habits, who has vainly tried to drill his whims and oddities to the regimental discipline of London life, and fire his opinions in platoons with the commonplace people of his parish, the moment he finds himself out of bounds of conventional tyranny, is sure to run into extremes. The English, consequently, pass for cracked on the continent of Europe, just as the Russians pass for *millionaires*; merely because the wealthy of Russia and eccentric of Great Britain are forced to travel in search of enjoyment.

Were they to stay at home, an inquest *de lunatico inquirendo* would soon settle the matter! The moment a presumptuous individual acts or thinks an inch out of the plumb-line of perpendicularity exacted by the formalities of society, his next of kin steps in to prove that he ate, drank, or slept at the hours that suited him, not at those which suited the rest of the world;—perhaps that he had an attachment to a particular coat, and wore it though threadbare, having new ones in his wardrobe;—or perhaps that he chose to have too many new ones in his wardrobe, though he had a good one to his back. Any twelve respectable steady jurymen, accustomed, like footmen, to their two suits a-year, and to eat, drink, and sleep by clockwork, will not hesitate to return him *non compos*; till the unhappy wretch is eventually driven into idiotcy by the imputed loss of reason.

An instance occurred a short time since of an individual, deprived of liberty and the control of his property by the decree of such a jury, and the evidence of the usual number of old women, who, being rational enough to give the slip to his incarcerators, figured with distinction at a foreign court, and obtained the verdict of the highest members of the French faculty that he not only possessed the use of his senses, but that his senses were of a highly intelligent order.

Had he lived in King Charles's days, or even in the days of the royal nieces of Charles, he would have been laughed at as an odd fellow, and perhaps hitched into a lampoon; or, fifty years later, mimicked in one of the farces of Foote. For, after all, what was he but one of the marked features of a varied surface of society? And when the cases of half the unfortunate persons we dismiss, as incompetent of mind, to a residence at Chiswick, Hanwell, or Hoxton, come to be investigated, it usually turns out that they are no odder than people who were called humourists in the days of Goldsmith, and characters in those of Fielding.

The great origin of this peremptory uniformity is the influence of our habits of business. To facilitate despatch, everything the least out of the common way must be avoided, and all obstacles in the railroad of life removed. People have no time to lose in wonder. They like to find in the man with whom they have to deal, a facsimile of themselves; so that they can meet him, point to point, without demur or examination. As society is at present constituted, they know to an item with what and whom they have to deal in a stockbroker, banker, physician or barrister. They could draw his portrait, or make a model of him, without ever having set eyes upon his face. Such people are made to pattern; and the type of each is as familiar to every mother's son of us, as though specifically sold at a turner's, like a bat and ball.

The classification of society has certainly effected a sort of overland-mailish facility of intercommunication between remote points of society. Lord Chancellors have become unmysterious as haberdashers; and my Lord Duke, no longer arrayed in his star, garter, and unapproachability, can be trafficked with in the sale of a hunter or a living, with as much ease as formerly his agent. The days of chain-mail and farthingales are gone by!—It is all Doudney,—all "rich gros de Naples at 1s. 11¾d. a yard!"

Epochs usually obtain a name in history, as the "age of gold," "the age of iron," "the age of the Crusades," "the age of Shakspeare;"—and Byron, in a fit of bitterness, characterized *our* century as "the age of bronze." The truth, and consequently the treason, would be far greater, were it defined as "the age of non-entityism!" Examine it in all its phases. Go to church, to the play, into the courts of law, nay, to court itself, and you will be forced to confess an utter want of individuality; and the Roman Emperor who wished that mankind had a single neck that he might make an end of it at a blow, should come back and see how vast a step we have achieved towards the accomplishment of his desire. To modify a phrase of Wordsworth, there are not "forty" but four millions "feeding like one!"

The oceanic platitude of such an order of existence is bad enough in itself; but even the least inquiring spectator cannot help exclaiming: What next? What became of Rome when it had drivelled into inanity? What became of France after the collapse into which it subsided after the over-excitement of the days of Louis le Grand? What shall we turn out after we have ceased to be a *bête monstre?* Shall we be parcelled out again, like the overgrown empire of Alexander? Or shall we rise up armed men, after being sown in the earth as the worn-out stumps of a dead dragon? Or are we fated to an eternal calm of corruption, like that described in the Ancient Mariner, when

> Slimy things did crawl with legs
> Upon the slimy sea?

After figuring as the infinitely little, are we become the infinitely less,—the *animalculæ* of modern civilization?

Time was, that comets were esteemed prodigies, and produced a national panic the moment their tails whisked into sight. But now that their movements are as well understood and correctly chronicled as those of the sober-sided fixed stars always winking in their proper places, people are delighted to be broken in upon by visitations which lend bloom to their roses and flavour to their vintage. Thanks to Van Amburgh and Carter, even lions and hyænas are tamed. Self-playing organs grind the oratorios of Handel into insignificance; and the Transfiguration of Raphael has lost its charm in the pale and worn-out lithographs which multiply and enfeeble its mysteries. The Seven wonders of the world are in ruins; and the only wonder left is that we cannot find out the secret of inventing an eighth.

Our ancestors ran to look at an aloe in bloom, believing that it flowered but once in a hundred years. *We* know better; but the aloe has lost its charm. Our ancestors reverenced the oaks that extended their gigantic arms beside their dwelling, certifying its antiquity far better than the genealogical tree in their hall. *We* bring ancient trees in Pickford's vans to our lawns, and make them overshadow our upstart villas; but the oak has lost its charm. Our ancestors thought a shilling well spent for admittance to see the skeleton of a cameleopard. *We* have giraffes giraffing unnoticed in the Regent's Park; and keep a serpentry for improving the domestic breed of rattlesnakes and boa constrictors. But if Mungo Park or Waterton were to write their Travels *now*, they would have lost their charm. The sting is taken out of everything: the flavour everywhere extracted!

Even the most high Court of Parliament mumbles where it used to bite. Its thunderbolts have fizzed into squibs: its storms are rattled with a sheet of iron and a quart of peas. People care no more about appearing at the bar of the Reformed House than at the bar of the Eagle Tavern. The terrors of the place have vanished. The Sultan, so terrible as the "turbaned Turk," is scarcely worth mentioning in a Fez!

Many persons still extant, must remember the villanous old coinage of George III; the tin-like sixpences which added a word to the slang dictionary, and the button-like shillings, of which the image and superscription might have been Caesar's or the Elector of Hanover's, for anything that the most scrutinising turnpikeman could decide to the contrary!—Just such flat and featureless dumps are we becoming. Nothing short of ringing on the counter can determine whether we be of the right metal.

It was held a national blessing when the Regent favoured us with a new coinage. For the first week or so, people scarcely liked to spend their half-crowns and shillings, so gloriously did they resemble medals. The inscriptions had to be read,—the reverses to be studied. The un-thrifty, who had flung about pursefuls of those bits of tin, began to hoard the new issue of the mint, as having more significance.

So will it be when the present generation gives place to a sharper die. The first man who dares to think and speak for himself, and think and speak strongly, will become as Gulliver in Lilliput. The prodigious flock of sheep into which it has pleased our nation to subside, will follow at his piping. Let him ply his galvanic battery with address, and the corpse of our defunct literature will revive; making, perhaps, like other galvanized corpses, a few grimaces in the onset.

Meanwhile a few sketches of men and women as they are, and were, in England, have been attempted in the following pages:— dissolving views of society,—too slight, let us hope, to provoke much severity of criticism.

Popular People

"THE SUCCESS OF CERTAIN WORKS maybe traced to sympathy between the author's mediocrity of ideas, and mediocrity of ideas on the part of the public!" observes a shrewd writer—evidently not a popular one, or he would entertain higher respect for the tribunal of public taste. It is certain, however, that, whether as regards books or men, there exists an excellence too excellent for general favour.

To make a hit, to captivate the public eye, ear, or understanding, without a certain degree of merit, is impossible. But it is not merit of the highest order that makes the hardest hit. Merit of the highest order must ever be "caviar to the general." The *chefs-d'œuvre* of art and literature are often condemned to years of obscurity; while some vulgar ballad seized upon by the barrel-organs, is made to persecute us in every street. Some coarse actor having convulsed the public with laughter by his buffooneries, the new farce becomes the darling of the public; and some familiar incident, from being daubed by the illustrative brush of a jocose artist, is lithographed into fame, and hung in all the inn parlours of the kingdom

So it is with human beings. Certain people as well as certain pieces obtain possession of the stage. Favoured guests as well as favoured pictures are to be found in every parlour. Talkers as well as tunes, may haunt one like a hand-organ in all directions; people whom every body likes,—whom every body invites,—and concerning whom everybody, when asked the motive of their liking, is sure to answer, "I like them because everybody likes them,—I like them because they are so popular."

The newspapers confer this arbitrary epithet upon their favourites as a species of diploma; "Mr. A., the popular poet," "Mr. B., the popular preacher," Mr. C., the popular member," "Mr. D., the popular actor," and so on through the alphabet. The greatest poets, preachers, and senators, have however been the least popular.

Society is apt to confer the honours of popularity upon lords and ladies, squires and squiresses, with partiality equally undiscriminating. Society dotes upon people who are neither so wise, so clever, so good, nor so great, as to afford too high a standard of wisdom or virtue, and consequently a tacit reproach to its own deficiencies. "Too good by half," "too clever by half," is a frequent phrase among those who are sneakingly conscious of being silly or worthless. They admit with a plausible air, that Mr. A.'s poetry, Mr. B.'s prose, or Mr. C.'s speeches, may be very fine for anything they know. But they do not pretend to understand them. With the same fatal smile of virtuous stupidity, they declare that, "A. is a superior man, certainly but nobody can bear him,—B. an accomplished woman, but singularly unpopular. While all the world admits the merits of the charming Mr. C. and Mrs. D.;—Mr. C. being so great an enlivenment to a dinner-party, and Mrs. D. a host in herself at Christmas in a country-house." Mr. C. and Mrs. D, are of course marked out for Popular People.

It is easy to understand how books may be puffed or nostrums advertised into popularity. Names that meet us in placards on every wall, or morning and evening in the columns of every newspaper, become, whether we will or no, engraven on our memory. We have all heard or read of Mallan's teeth, Solomon's spectacles, Mechi's razor-strops, or Stocken's envelopes. We have seen them praised till we begin to have some faith in their virtues. We cannot believe that so much printer's ink and advertisement duty would be expended for nothing. But it is much more difficult to comprehend how "the world's large tongue" can be bribed to wag in favour of such very small deer as the Mr. Cs and Mrs. Ds.

"A sop to Cerberus," is the ordinary way of stopping the bark and bite of the infernal monster. But that "many-headed monster thing," the public, is a Cerberus requiring such a perpetual supply of sops, that the effort seems supernatural.

The truth is that popularity resembles certain echoes which, once evoked, repeat themselves *ad infinitum*. If anyone can be found to utter the phrase or praise loud enough in the first instance, it proceeds in the sequel to repeat itself, after the fashion of the courtiers in Count Hamilton's charming story of "Fleur d'Epine."

We are wrong, perhaps, to say "anyone;" for the privilege of bestowing popularity is specific with certain persons. Let the dullest book ever written be praised in a certain review—it will sell; let the dullest dog that ever prosed be proclaimed an able man by a certain coterie,—he will become a popular talker. We have more than one charming Countess who has only to pronounce a man a *bel esprit*, to stamp his popularity at all the dinners of the season; we have more than one *valseur* at Almack's, who has only to dance twice with the same *débutante,* to render her the most popular partner in the ball-rooms of May Fair.

In such trivial distinctions as these, indeed, it is not surprising that the world should be credulous. But in matters that concern its welfare,—its existence here and hereafter,—its mortal body,—its immortal soul!—To let the pretty prattlers or elephantine prosers of society, create the popular physician,—the popular preacher!

The nambypamby of the popular poet may be laid on the shelf. But through the blunders of the popular physician we may come to be laid out,—or laid in the grave; while the errors of the popular preacher may induce a still more alarming consummation. Through the combined agency of both, we may, as Don Juan says,—but what Don Juan says is not always fit to be repeated.

"*Do* send for Dr. Creaksley, my dear," cries the Dowager Lady Gunderton, one of the most accredited popularity-mongers of modern society. "Creaksley is the only man going,—Creaksley is the person who performed such a miracle for Lord Growley's child, by saving its life after it had been immersed five minutes in a cauldron of boiling water. He had it kept in a bath of iced camphorated oil a day and a night. Ah! Creaksley is a wonderful man. He has three pair of carriage-horses always on the trot, and never takes his own horses off the stones. During the season there are always posters waiting for Creaksley at Hyde-park-corner, to take him to the fashionable villas. One can't get him without three days' notice. Since the days of the famous Dr. Radcliffe, never was physician so popular!"

And why?—What is the origin of this wondrous popularity which keeps coach-horses on the trot, and dowagers on the gabble?—Is it skill, learning, knowledge, tact, experience? By no means!— Creaksley is a man of trivial mind, and equable temperament; patient with his patients, hospitable with his acquaintances;— who, if he let people die, never kills them by the rashness of his experiments;—and when he allows them to live, does not render life a bore. Creaksley talks agreeably, because wise enough to talk of anything but physic; which he would probably throw to the dogs, if he thought the dogs foolish enough to take it. Far easier to administer it at a guinea a dose to such ninnies as the Dowager Lady Gunderton, seeing that the Dowager Lady Gunderton is able to promote his apotheosis as a popular physician.

Then there is Sir Gordon Mosley! With what party does one ever dine throughout the London season without meeting Sir Gordon Mosley?—Sir Gordon Mosley is as inevitable as the tongue and chickens,—or the turbot and lobster sauce. Sir Gordon Mosley and his white cravat are essential portions of every well-mounted dinner-table. People expect to meet him with as dead a certainty as sherry or champagne.

Read the dinner lists of the Morning Post; one could almost fancy there were half-a-dozen Sir Gordon Mosleys, so infallibly is he comprised in each one of them. "The Marquis of H. entertained a distinguished party at dinner on Monday last, including the Prince of Rigmaroli Fuggi, the Earl and Countess of Mungewell, Sir Gordon Mosley, and other distinguished guests."—"The Chancellor of the Exchequer entertained at dinner, on Tuesday last, the Master of the Rolls, Viscount and Viscountess Trimmer, Lord Hobbledehoy, Lord Grig, Sir Gordon Mosley, and a large and distinguished circle."—We find Sir Gordon Mosley in the

Court Circular:—we find him in the company of Lord Chancellor, archbishops, judges, princes, peers, academicians, presidents of all sorts of colleges, authors, and ministers of state.—Sir Gordon Mosley is ubiquitous—Sir Gordon Mosley is universal.

Sometimes on arriving late for a dinner-party, you look round the circle assembled in the drawing-room, miss him, and congratulate yourself that for once you have escaped. Don't flatter yourself!—Five minutes before the announcement of dinner you will find that he has glided in, and is whispering behind the chair of your hostess. Sir Gordon Mosley knows the habits of every dining-house in town, and can calculate to a turn the arrival of the guests, and roasting of the venison. He is not only there, but there to a minute.

Strangers are naturally anxious to ascertain the peculiar merit of this integral fraction of the eating world. At table, they lend an attentive ear to his conversation,—in the drawing-room they fix an observant eye on his deportment. "Where be his quips, his quirks, his flashes of merriment?"—or if not his wit, where is his wisdom,—where his information?

Worthy public! Sir Gordon Mosley is a moral non-entity; a man who knows nothing, save where he is to dine to-morrow, and next day, and every day of the week. He has a good countenance, wears a good coat, bears a good name, makes a good bow, is civil and conciliating, of a medium tint that harmonises with everybody; one in short, who, without one faculty or quality of real distinction, retains a high place in the category of Popular People.

Mr. Meggot is a gentleman equally important in the estimation of the coteries—not as a diner out—for his name is less grandiloquent in the announcement of the butler, or lists of the Morning Post; but for the *soirée* or squeeze. Meggot is a something in his way. He sat through two Sessions in parliament, where he said nothing; and was Secretary of Legation at some foreign Court, where he *did* nothing. But he is a man ever to be seen at the elbow of ministers, or button-held by the leading men of the day. The cabinet sets a high value on him. The doctrinarians (for England has its sect of doctrinarians as well as France), look up to him with respect. Meggot's name is cited as an endorsement to an opinion, like Rothschild's to a loan; and when Meggot is stated not to be much shocked at any occurrence, the world decides that it cannot be very dreadful.

This, at least, *must* be a superior man. This authority, to which sages and states men bow, must be a true oracle. An oracle?—Meggot is a man who, in the whole course of his existence, never uttered an opinion—Meggot is an echo,—an embodied affirmative, the best listener in the world. He is one of those who submit to be told the things he knows, by people who know nothing about the matter. He is ready to swallow the most monstrous assertions. He seems convinced by the most preposterous arguments. His air of candour is worth a million. When we reflect upon the craving appetite of human vanity, it is not wonderful that such a man should command the affections of society, and stand pre-eminent in the ranks of Popular People.

Sporus enjoys a less gratuitous species of popularity;—Sporus is a popular author. His works flash upon one like Lucifer matches, and go off like detonating guns. No sooner in print, than out of print. The reviews revere him,—the daily papers delight in him,— the magazines make much of him. Nothing like Sporus!—Such style—such delicacy—such freedom from affectation! The *petite maîtresse* buys him and binds him up in morocco; the school-mistress buys him and binds him up in calf; the bookseller buys him and binds him up in a penalty to complete a new book at a month's warning. Great guns are discharged from the battery of the press on the production of every new work, as on the birth of the sons of the Sultan. He is written up, till one fears that the sky must be raised a story to make way for his renown. The most crabbed of critics grows mild in treating of him; and the reading world, like Monsieur Laffarge, is poisoned in doses of sugar and water.

And who or what is this successor of Scott and Byron? This Hallam, this Rogers, this Moore?—Alas! Sporus is but a shadow of his namesake of the days of Pope:—

A mere white-curd of ass's milk;

or rather, the mere mouldy sponge of a leaden inkstand.

But Sporus excites no jealousies—Sporus eclipses no humiliated rival. Sporus is one of whom literary men say with a smile among themselves, "Poor Sporus! he is painstaking writer, and really an excellent fellow. Let us do him a good turn."

Puffed, therefore, and praised on all sides, his writings first attract notice, and finally command attention. The public is convinced that *all* the weekly, monthly, and three-monthly critics cannot be in the wrong. The public asks for his picture,—the public demands his bust. The public will one day ask a pension for him from Government; and eventually, perhaps, from the Dean and chapter of Westminster, a corner in Westminster Abbey. Is not *this* placing poor, harmless Sporus in the catalogue of Popular People?

Concerning the popularity of the numskulls who give feasts that wise men may eat them, no one need to express surprise. The popularity of proprietors of hospitable country-houses, is equally comprehensible; so is the popularity of East-India Directors.

> Long live all those who've anything to give,

is the cry of many besides the luckless poet in whose mouth it was wickedly placed by James and Horace Smith.

But Lady Creepmouse has nothing to give, not even a dinner!— Lady Creepmouse has no country-house; Lady Creepmouse has a wretched house in town. She is not handsome—she is not young—she is not rich—she is not clever.—Yet no one even names her, except as that charming Lady Creepmouse!

Would you know the origin of this extraordinary popularity? It is because—but no! On this one occasion, let us be discreet; on this one occasion, let us be merciful. We have no quarrel with Lady Creepmouse. Let her sun herself while she can in the smiles of the world; enjoying to their utmost limit the pleasures and immunities accorded to Popular People.

The Gossip

WHY ARE THE ENGLISH—the grave English—the intellectual English—the moral English—the greatest gossips in the world? No one conversant with the social life of other nations, will deny the fact;—but who will adduce the cause? Doctor Johnson defines to gossip "to chat, to spend time idly." A more correct definition of the word, as used in modern parlance, would be, "to spend time idly in chatting of other peoples' affairs."

Yet the English are not a people addicted to spending time idly. It must be some overmastering influence that inspires them with the vague curiosity leading to so vile a waste of the impalpable treasure more precious than silver or gold.

Is it that the desire of knowledge, so extensively cultivated among us by the high-pressure power of modern education, begets in weak minds, incapable of retaining solid information, a restless craving after intelligence? Does learning, like the wind which extinguishes a candle while it stimulates a great fire, strengthen the strong mind, but enfeeble the weak? No matter!— By some defect of organization, the English, taken as a mass, are decided gossips. Is it not written in the book of the chronicles of their public journals—those bulletins of the national mind? Is it not attested by the avidity with which the most trivial anecdotes of domestic life are circulated and eagerly swallowed, by that yawning gulf, the reading public? Is it not pointed out with a sneer by the foreign world,—rejoicing to detect in our details of private parties and descriptions of court-trains and feathers, a counterbalance to the sageness of our councils, and vastness of our scientific achievements?

The scandal of personality is put down in continental countries by the strong arm of the law; but the froth of every-day "fashionable intelligence," is simply blown aside by the contemptuous lips, of common sense!

But it is the appetite for gossip, and not the food which the yearnings of that appetite bring into the market, with which we have to deal. The press gossips for society, because society gossips for itself and makes no secret of its love of gossiping, on pretence that a mere tattler is a merely harmless person. But the taste thus established, is any thing but harmless. Like the bind-weed, which, when suffered to take root, extinguishes the growth of more profitable plants, it intertwines itself irretrievably with all the produce of the soil.

Critics boast of a new work as "a pleasant gossiping book;"— people boast of a new acquaintance, as "a pleasant gossiping fellow;" and the most valuable of our periodicals was a few years ago redeemed from decadence by a series of "pleasant gossiping articles." Without pretending to excessive wisdom or exorbitant morality, without being arrayed

> in a gown and band,
> Just to entitle one to make a fuss,

it may fairly be asserted that this fashion of erecting into a virtue that which is a mere weakness, is unworthy the pastors and masters of the public mind. The sketcher of modern character, is an especial sufferer from the evil. To avoid the vagueness of describing, like Theophrastus, "The absent man," "The miser," he assigns, after the example of La Bruyère, imaginary names to his creations. A Dr. Creaksley or Sir Gordon Mosley, appears more likely to grapple with the fancy of the reader than "The fashionable physician" or "The diner out." Forthwith, the gossips begin to bristle their manes and lash their tails. From house to house runs the confidential whisper of "Have you seen the sketch of A.?" "What think you of the portrait of B.?" "Creaksley, you know, is A.; and Sporus (how shameful!) is B!"—

Yet Creaksley, courteous reader, is as much A., or Sporus B., as Danneker's Ariadne is a personal portrait of Bacchus's "loved and left of old;" or as Guido's Aurora may be called a picture of the rosy morn. Types of a class, it affords evidence of their accuracy that originals are so readily supplied and strenuously pointed out for these airy outlines. But it also affords proof of the truth of what we have already advanced,—that England, and more especially London, is an abominable gossip!—When a new work of fiction issues from the press, in a style called by the French *un roman de mœurs*, by ourselves, a fashionable novel, be sure that it is either personal, or will pretend to be personal, or will be said to be personal. Without some such *nota bene* to the Gossips, the piquancy of its general hits at the foibles of society would be thrown away. At this very moment, half our readers are running on impatiently through our page, hoping that some especial Gossip, male or female, will be pointed out to shame, and some entertaining anecdote cited, in order to fasten the label round the right neck! "Have at ye all, my gossips!"—Not *one* of you, ladies, but is the original of the horrible Lady Pagginton we are about to describe; not *one* of you, gentlemen, but has your sympathetic part in "that amusing, gossiping fellow," Flutter, of whom more anon.

You are all gossips! You gossip every where, of every thing;—not alone of the dinner-party and ball-room,—the pink satin dress and flirtation in the balcony;—but after visiting a condemned cell, you gossip concerning the morose anguish of the being you have beheld contemplating the terrors of eternity!—You obtain an order for Bethlem Hospital: and, unawed by the spectacle of one of the overmaster in scourges of the human race, garnish your discourse at the gay dinner-table with pleasant anecdotes of the comicalities of madmen!—You see to the factory, and after shuddering at the blue faces and pinched noses of the suffering population, return home and gossip pleasantly at the conversazione concerning the curious dialect of the overseer, or the quaint comments of some droll little victim promoted to the honours of interrogation.

An infirm nobleman is murdered at dead of night in his chamber. With what hosts of entertaining anecdotes, and clever puns do the gossips recount the narrative of his assassination!—A woman elopes from her husband, leaving her infants motherless; what joy for the gossips in all the concomitant details of the wig and broken spectacles of the paramour! On such occasions, regardless of the influence of such histories on their own minds and the minds of their hearers, the gossips overrun both town and country, scattering the seeds of their tares in all directions.

The most awful catastrophes—suicide, battle, murder, sudden death—become reduced to the same trifling consistency—the same chaff—after being ground in the mill and winnowed through the sieve of a gossip.

Be patient, gentle reader: we promised you "a light gossiping article." You shall come to Lady Pagginton and Felix Flutters in time. Allow us, however, to begin with the gossip of an humbler sphere.

There is Miss Bargeham, the favourite milliner of the well-known market-place of B. ("B?—B. certainly stands for Birmingham!" murmurs some gossiping reader). For the last thirty years, the counters of Kitty Bargeham have obtained a remarkable preference over a succession of new comers in the immediate neighbourhood. Vainly have the windows of her rivals displayed the most unquestionable superiority of cap and turban, hat and bonnet, plaid ribbons and Chantilly veils. These parti-coloured attractions have invariably given place with in the year to a placard of "To Let, Unfurnished;" or, "To be Sold under Prime Cost, by Order of the Assignees." One rash firm even went as far as to advertise the attraction of a Parisian assistant. "A young lady from the eminent French house of Mesdames Follette et Cie, Rue Vivienne."—In vain!—In six months, the shop was shut up and the Parisian assistant shut out. There was no standing against the "light gossiping articles" of Kitty Bargeham.

Oh! that back-parlour!—Oh! the inedited anecdotes of Brush Park and Lark Hall, conveyed from their respective ladies' maids, to the ears of the milliner, and from the milliner to the ears of all the trades men's wives and farmers' daughters of the neighbourhood of B.! The shoe-ribbon purchased of Mesdames Brown, or the green veil of Mrs. Smith, might be of worthier texture, or even by sixpence a better bargain. But what was that compared with the joy of having been seated face to face with Kitty Bargeham, in her little stuffy, dingy sanctum, listening to charming inuendos about Sir Thomas Lark's London losses at play; or hints that "something would be sure to come of Miss Melusinda Brush's early walks in the green lane." Kitty "knew it from the best authority,"—but Kitty "would say no more!"

More reputations were "done to death by slanderous tongues" in Kitty Bargeham's back-parlour, than in the whole county besides;—a perpetual twitter of chit-chat being emitted on every opening of its sacred door, to tantalize the less privileged customers not yet initiated into the gossip-shop. But Brush Park is now to be let, and Lark Hall to be sold; too hot to hold the respective proprietors, martyrized *à coup d'épingles* by the milliner of the market-place.

Lady Pagginton—(draw your chair closer to the fender, courteous gossip,—we have got to Lady Pagginton at last!—) is a widow, and a London lady,—that is, a Marylebonian, the most diluted and colourless species of the London lady. Mediocrity personified, whether as regards mind, body or estate, Lady P. has managed to make herself heard of as the gnats do—by humming and stinging. The creature means no harm—'tis in its nature. But the sting is not the less irritating, nor the noise less tiresome. So is it with Lady P. Her perseverance in making her way into your house, her perseverance in communicating in emphatic whispers idle sayings concerning still idler doings in which you have not the slightest interest, her perseverance in attributing to her last auditor the comments with which she has herself embroidered the intelligence derived from her first informant, are worthy a better cause. You might cut a canal with almost half the labour.

Nothing too great, nothings too little, to be caught up and carried off in her ladyship's budget. To the little matters, like the bits of worthless glass which acquire beauty in a kaleidoscope, she imparts importance by a species of scientific illusion; while the great ones she brings within her paltry compass, as the body of

De Rancé's mistress was forced into the leaden coffin, by cutting off the head. She contrives to gossip about the affairs of the East, by garnishing them with secret anecdotes of our lady of Cairo, the renowned widow of Mehemet Ali's eldest son; or sets her mark upon the politicians of the West, by rumours pilfered from the Charivari, about the domestic life of a minister, whose whole life is public; or the secret cabinet of Metternich, through whose keyhole not even the winds of heaven are permitted to whistle.

But without this mischievous occupation, this perpetual cobbling of colloquial shreds and patches, what would become of the vapid, unmeaning, unconnected Lady P.? Devote her leisure to some useful purpose?—Condescend to knit—sew—read? Why, she would sink into a second-rate person of respectability; losing all pretext for intruding upon your more serious occupations, in her capacity of "a most lively, agreeable woman, knowing everybody, full of anecdote; in short, the very perfection of A GOSSIP!"

Felix Flutter is a more dangerous individual. His story and note savour of the rattlesnake rather than the gnat; *his* smatterings consist of steel-filings rather than of chaff; *his* pourings forth are *aqua Tofana*, rather than milk-and-water; but all dispensed under the same delusive head, of "light, pleasant gossip!"

Men might be brought to the scaffold, or condemned to the cart, for the crimes, "pleasant but wrong," imputed in the light anecdotes which Flutter impels like shuttle-cocks from his smart racket, from house to house. Like the snake-charmers of the East, who amuse your leisure with the display of reptiles, that seem to curl and play in their adroit hands, he ties love-knots with adders! Worse still, when, like the cunning seers of Egypt, who, by pretended incantations, seem to withdraw from beneath the very cushions of your divan, the serpent they have cunningly introduced into the chamber to accredit their power, Felix Flutter contrives to inspire your mind with terror and mistrust, by ascribing to the treachery of a bosom friend, the mischief concocted by his own malice!

But Flutter is such an amusing fellow! Nothing like him for a morning visit—a dull dinner-party! Like Mr. Merryman, at

Gyngell's, his pockets are always full of squibs and crackers, to be discharged at intervals, when the wit of the company runs low.

And then he is so plausible! His most improper little stories make their appearance in the most decent attire: like one of Congreve's gallants, arrayed in the gown and cassock of Dr. Spintext; or Cartouche, dressed up as one of the Maréchaussée to rob a house. Nothing more decorous—nothing more deadly. He runs you through the body with a regulation small-sword; or if you insist on committing suicide, sells you your arsenic, with "poison" labelled on the packet, as per order of the Magistrates' Bench.

My public! know ye not this Felix Flutter?—Has he not related, *sub rosa*, of each of you to the other, that your grandfathers were one shocking thing, and your grand mothers the other shocking thing?—That you have overdrawn your banker—that you have injured your early friends—that you have blasphemed the church—or conspired against the state?—Know ye not Felix Flutter?—Know'ye not *ten* Felix Flutters—*twenty* Felix Flutters?—Know ye not, in short, in some shape or other, the concentrated essence of A MODERN GOSSIP?

Susceptible People

THE INCOMPARABLE CHARLES LAMB USED to fancy he could detect a schoolmaster by his grammatical scrupulosities in the use of the subjunctive mood. But for the fear of the said schoolmaster before our eyes, we should have headed this article, "Touchy People," according to the popular phrase. Pedantically speaking, the word should be "Tetchy;" and so, to steer clear between plain English and pure English, we have taken leave to Anglicise the French designation of those self who are ever suspecting or resenting affronts; thin-skinned martyrs, "tremblingly alive all o'er" to ideal injuries, or wincing, like other galled jades, under imaginary lashes.

A sketch of these gratuitous martyrs forms a natural appendage to the gossip; since to their mutual reaction, the weakness of the one and the power of the other is chiefly attributable. The mischief-making of the gossip renders silly people susceptible; the susceptibility of the foolish, encourages the gossip to play upon their infirmity of character.

There is no stronger symptom of insignificance, than to be touchy! The moment a person's position is definite, he ceases to be anxious concerning the slights of society; while those by birthright placed above the little impertinences of the little, are incapable of surmising the possibility of affront. Susceptibility on such points, is an almost unfailing symptom of *a raw*.

There is some reason that we know not of, why Lady Manly should resent her visit not being returned with sufficient celerity;

there is some latent motive for the flush that overspreads poor Mordaunt's brow, when unable to catch Lord Cecil's eye for a bow, at the theatre. We should not have set ourselves to the task of inquiring why the notice of such people was important to them, but for their resentment of an offence, after all, perhaps, imaginary. It is like a man scudding along a wall, in the consciousness that his coat is out at elbows. "Ne faut pas parler de corde dans la maison d'un pendu!" says a French adage; and when we see a man resent an allusion to Tyburn, we have a right to suppose that the rope has acted its part in the family history.

Be this a hint to susceptible people, lest their infirmity of temper expose them to unjust suspicions. "I am certain he was talking at *me*!"—"That show up was at my expense!" are phrases serving as finger-posts to secret infirmities. How should we know that Mrs. Dove was overbearing in her *ménage*, but for her insisting that she was caricatured in the heroine of some shrew-contemning novel? —How conjecture that Colonel Lawless had exhibited the better part of valour in the Burmese war, but for his calling out some lawyer's clerk for jesting, in his presence, upon the white feather?

Some people consider this sort of susceptibility an amiable weakness; and apologise for having been cold or ungracious without a cause, on the score of their "foolish sensitiveness." Foolish, indeed—*worse* than foolish. Touchiness is one of the most paltry phases of egotism and vanity. It is only those with whom self is ever upper most, who dream of being touchy. There are some persons so singularly constituted, that, go where they may, do what they will, their own shadow, grown gigantic, seems projected before them, as if to convict them of a perpetual attempt to eclipse the sun. They can see nothing in nature but themselves. Every thing said, thought, written by the rest of the world, must bear reference to *them*. The result is, that the rest of the world becomes unanimous in thinking them insupportable.

Conscious of unpopularity, they live in terror of slight. As it is impossible that others should appreciate them at the inordinate value they set upon themselves, they must find themselves disparaged. They must experience the affront of seeing precedence given to the Duke of Wellington for valour, and Luttrell for wit. Try to get at the origin of some author's animosity towards you, and you will learn that you took the liberty of doing justice to Bulwer in his presence, when you must have known that such exaggerated praise of a rival could not be agreeable. Or inquire the motive of Lady Ridlemaree's omitting you from her last ball,—you will be told that you offended her, by giving due praise to the serene loveliness of Lady Jocelyn. Wounded vanity is the true origin of all touchiness.

To public men, this infirmity is a serious disqualification. Susceptibility in such cases amounts to an admission of vulnerability; it is the act of publishing by sound of trumpet the exact measure of his strength, or rather of his weakness.

A touchy man, in the House of Commons, sets himself up as a target. The young members delight in taking a rise out of him. It is a sort of badger-bait for the lovers of illegitimate sport. Such men are always starting up, or launching out, under the influence of whips and stings from invisible hands, like Caliban capering under the impish inifictions of Prospero. Their bodies, like that of the son of Sycorax, are filled with pains and aches. But where is the enemy?—Every where!—They see their tormentors in the smooth face that smiles upon them, and expect an agonizing gripe from the friendly hand extended towards their own!

Public men have died,—ay! actually died, and the worms have eaten them—from the influence of this morbid susceptibility. Not merely by bringing quarrels upon themselves to be decided at the rapier's point; but under the influence of slights attributed by their touchiness to their sovereign, or ingratitude, to the nation. The perpetual hair-shirt of wounded self-love has eventually worn out their constitution. Touchiness sends great men to the tomb, just as it sends lesser ones to Coventry.

If the foolish and vulgar enjoyed a monopoly of this painful frailty, we might say, "let them fancy that the windmills are making war upon them—no matter!" But, unluckily, touchiness is also one of the follies of the wise. Read Pope's correspondence; consult the Memoirs of Swift; turn over the pages of Scaliger;

listen to the howlings of Warburton; reflect upon the miseries of Shenstone, touchy, not only for himself, but for his Leasowes. Above all, Rousseau:—Rousseau's life was a never-ending warfare against imaginary insults. From the Pope down to the gentle duchesses on whose knees like a spoiled child he was cherished, all were aggressors. The eloquent and enlightened Jean Jacques, in his bursts of irritability and touchiness, betrayed himself as belonging to the class described by himself as "n'ayant pas en elles ce fonds de tendresse qui fait accepter l'imperfection de l'être humain—ces personnes qui sont bonnes et affectueuses seulement quand elles rêvent." In his writings, he was a philosopher; in real life, a petulant child!

Nothing appears more troublesome to individuals, who, on their own side, are possessed of this *fonds de tendresse*—this generous disposition, this forbearance, this tendency to live and let live,—than to find themselves in contact with those less lavishly endowed, who are continually imagining causes for dissension, and displaying wounds to be salved over.

People so thinskinned that every little rub produces a gangrene, cease at length to excite commiseration. Let their qualities be what they may, others, of inferior merit, who are more *facile à vivre*, will be preferred as companions. However exciting the sport, to fish in troubled waters becomes, in the long run, tedious. We like to feel sure when about to meet an old friend, whether he is likely to fold us in his arms, or run us through the body. We tired of even the most favoured correspondent, who is always signing himself "the madly-used Malvolio." We prefer stars of inferior magnitude, if less liable to conceal themselves by fits and starts in the clouds. We choose our friends to be what the French call *d'un commerce sûr*. Equality of humour, the equality proceeding from a fair estimate of our own claims, and a generous estimate of those of others, is in social life an indispensable qualification.

The offence, however, carries its own penalty. The man who is always fancying that you "bite your thumb at *him*,"—the man, who, to borrow Hood's most piquant simile,

—to his own sharp fancies a prey,
Lies like a hedgehog, roll'd up the wrong way,
Tormenting himself with his prickles,

is more to be pitied, than if those prickles were the spears of an enemy. His enemy could not be *always* a-tilt for single combat; but at what hour of the twenty-four is the monomaniac safe from his own antagonism? Like Harpagon, he seizes himself by the arm, as the robber who has despoiled him of his treasure!

And then the mortification to a touchy person of having it proved to him that he has been fencing with a shadow;—the vexation of having to own himself in the wrong. And how easy to deceive ourselves concerning the attacks made upon our self-love! Many years ago, the writer of these sketches produced at Drury Lane Theatre a comedy, entitled "Lords and Commons," in which that excellent comedian, William Farren, enacted the part of an old Nabob, admirably costumed, according to his conception of the part. Immediately on his entrance, a murmur of disapprobation arose, for which at the moment it was difficult to assign a motive. The following day, several newspaper critics noticed with regret that the part should have been dressed at a well-known individual, noted for his harmless eccentricities, &c., &c., while more familiar friends exclaimed, "a shameful show up of JEREMEY BENTHAM!—The wig, especially, was a facsimile!"

The comedy and the wig were soon afterwards laid on the shelf together. But to this day, a warm devotee of old Jeremy continues to reproach us with the treachery of our attack upon "an eminent old man, who ought to have been an object of respect to a young writer."

Mr. Bunn's amusing "Memoirs of the Stage" threw new light upon the matter. The wig in question was fated to become as much an object of contention as the lock of Mrs. Arabella Fermor's hair, the origin of the charming poem of Pope.

On the appearance of Scribe's brilliant comedy of "Bertrand et Raton," under the name of "The Minister and the Mercer," general indignation was excited in the royal and ministerial circles, by the appearance of Farren in the part of the ambitious intriguant, in a wig said to be a facsimile of the one worn by Talleyrand at the Congress of Vienna!—

The King signified his displeasure to the Lord Chamberlain— the Lord Chamberlain to the manager—the manager to the imprudent histrion. It was by no means certain that a rupture between England and France might not be the result of this insult offered to the French Ambassador. Lord Grey, then at the head of the administration, attended at the theatre to verify the delinquency.

The offending wig thus resented by his Majesty's Government as an offence to good order, and sworn to by hundreds as a deliberate copy from the peculiar and well-known head-dress of Talleyrand, was the identical one worn in the part of Sir Caleb Cabob, and also sworn to by scores as a caricature of Jeremy Bentham!—So much for the accuracy of peoples impressions on such points. So much for the folly of taking to oneself a random shot!

There is a man who would be clever and agreeable but for the solitary foible of touchiness, who "dies daily" from the self-appropriation of random shots. He fancies himself the object of every whisper, every smile, every caricature, every joke circulated in the circle of his acquaintance! Sir John Sensitive once gained a contested election, and kept his bed for six weeks afterwards, from the severe wounds inflicted by the ordinary squibs of the hustings. Sir John Sensitive once paid his court to the prettiest woman in his county, and was on the eve of acceptance; when her ladyship happening to say, in his presence, that she disliked lawyers, he drew off and took affront, because his great-grandfather happened to have been Master of the Rolls. Sir John Sensitive has fought three duels; one with his bosom friend for joking with him about a grammatical fault in his pamphlet on Catholic Emancipation; one with the member for his county on the strength of his allusion in parliament to certain landowners of intolerant principles in the large and populous county he had the honour to represent; and the third, with a gentleman of distinguished merit and talent, whom he persisted in mistaking for H.B., just as he had persisted in mistaking himself for the original of one of the clever *croquis* of that successful caricaturist.

Sweet Sir John! be warned.—The last bullet of the Freischutz may await thee.

> Three have proved true—
> The fourth thou mayst rue

Take patience!—The world is wide enough to allow even so great a man to pass unnoticed. Conquer thy perilous irritabilities, and rise superior to the weakness of those pigmies on stilts, whom we have designated under the name of SUSCEPTIBLE PEOPLE.

Plausible People

I N SOCIETY, AS IN THE arts, as in literature, as in politics, or in
fifty other things,

> The world is still deceived by ornament.

Not alone by gems of price, "barbaric gold and pearl;"—but
by Birmingham gilding as well as barbaric gold,—by glass beads
as well as orient pearl. Though aware that "there be counterfeits
abroad," we accept people on their own showing; albeit that
showing bear as much proportion to the reality, as the portrait of
a dwarf or giant placed before a booth at a fair, to the tall man or
short woman exhibiting within!

It is a favourite jest with the French that you may knock a man
down, provided you preface the offence with the word "pardon!"
or, as the song runs,

> qu'on peut tout faire,
> Quand on le fait *poliment*!

In England, you may do what you like, provided you do it
plausibly. Cant your way through life, with the seven deadly
sins in your train, not asserting them to be angels, but wishing
to goodness they were not quite so wicked, and humbly hoping
that some day or other they may see the error of their ways, and

you will pass for a heavenly-minded man. Deprecation, whether in tone, manner, or phraseology, is an universal pass-key. There is no knowing exactly where to convict such sinners. They envelop themselves in such a thick coating of sackcloth and ashes, that there is some difficulty in finding out the vulnerable points. Their hypocrisy is a sort of shifting shield, which, like the sails of a windmill, veer with your attack, and protect them in whatever direction they are approached.

According to Rochefoucault's definition of a courtier, "*un homme sans humeur et sans honneur*," they never suffer themselves to be provoked out of their plausible equanimity. Ever gracious, ever placable, their humility is that of Tartuffe, their impassibility that of Talleyrand, who would not allow the person with whom he was conversing to discover, by the expression of his countenance, that he had received a kick from his enemy in the rear.

To this *sub*-human patience, however, they superadd more active propensities. The plausible person is essentially a talking animal,—an ambulatory puff,—an utterer of vauntings—"not loud, but deep." He accuses himself in the humblest tone of being guilty of all the cardinal virtues.

According to his own account, the circumstances attending *his* conduct are invariably extenuating. "He does not wish to praise himself," but he labours under the singular impunity attributed to the right divine of the throne: he can do no wrong. By some strange concatenation of events, he is impeccable. It would grieve him much that he should be supposed to pride himself on this. Heaven forbid that he should be pharisaical in his virtue. On the contrary, humility has been esteemed his leading merit. But so it is, that when others fall into frailty, by some inherent quality (such as the leaden foundation of a Dutch tumbler), he is *forced* to stand up right.

The world, that wide-mouthed dupe, swallows all this as glibly as it is uttered. The man who anoints himself all over with the oil of laudation above his fellows, may pass through the eye of a needle, albeit as crooked as a camel. Smooth as a billiard-ball, and sticking at nothing, he makes his infallible way into the pocket, and secures the game. *His* is the virtue which, so far from being its own reward, obtains a premium from parliament, and sets itself up like a golden image for the adoration of the multitude.

Plausible people are the fatted kine of this world. They insinuate themselves like the weasel into the meal-tub; or like Reynard, their stealthy steps make an unsuspected way into the hen-roost. While your ears are still fascinated by their gentle protestations, you find they have been picking your locks, or your pocket. While the patriot praises himself for more than Spartan virtue, he is watching your eye for a favourable opportunity to escape up the back stairs, and sneak into the presence of royalty.—The next time you see him he will be on the Treasury Bench!

Another favourite form of plausibility, is to appear in the arena of life, trembling and defenceless, "*sans armes comme l'innocence,*"

> a naked new-born babe,
> Striding the blast.

You cannot tread upon a thing that crawls at your feet, and calls itself a worm. If it owned itself an asp, you would have a right to exterminate the reptile. "But a poor, harmless, miserable, unoffending worm, that could not do mischief if it would, and would not if it could, you would not be such a monster as to set your foot upon its innocent head."

Thus pleaded for by its own weakness, the worm of Nile establishes itself by your hearth; and one fine day, when you find yourself stung with mortal venom, the fatal wound proves to have proceeded from "the poor, harmless, miserable, unoffending worm, that could not do mischief if it would, and would not if it could!" Where upon you utter a few uncourteous remarks concerning Plausible People.

The force of endeavour will do wonders towards acquiring the form and show of righteousness, by those who

> Assume a virtue though they have it not.

In the crowd of beggars that surround a travelling-carriage at the foreign post-houses, some halt, some blind, some maimed— all screaming for charity,—it requires the eye of a policeman to detect the genuine cripple, and make the dumb speak. If the uninitiated pretend to perform Duke Humphry's miracle, and make the lame man fling aside his crutches, and fly the field, they are sure to hit upon the wrong man, so cunning are the impostors. So is it with the Plausible. By dint of strenuously pretending to be good, wise, or zealous, they contract almost the form and pressure of virtue and wisdom. A jeweller could scarcely detect the pure gold from the crysocal. Though we positively know that it is the clown preaching in the sacerdotal robe of Sir Topaz, we cannot help listening with reverence to his exposition of the doctrines of the Metempsychosis. He looks so *very* grave—he talks so *very* learnedly! Our prejudices must have deceived us. The man so very like the chaplain, cannot be the fool!

Above all, it is scarcely possible to detect a plausible woman. Had Messalina chosen to array herself in a vestal's robe, and take her part in the procession as a bearer of the sacred fire, by due gravity of deportment she would have secured the respect of the multitude. So, in our own times, a quaker's dress is the favourite disguise of the least reputable frequenters of masquerades; and enormous professions of morality form the distinguishing feature of belles of higher degree who have lapses of honour to conceal behind that whited wall.

It is only in a faint whisper that the select few who listen to their chantings, insinuate that "the lady doth protest too much;"—that such very strait-lacing usually purports to disguise imperfection in the shape.—The world, edified by her precepts of holiness, her *suspirium sanctorum*, cries "Hear, hear, hear," with all its lungs; and makes affidavit that the Venus de Medicis is not more free from deformity than the Sheldrake-invented form which so sweetly solicits approbation. How indeed should the public be savage, when addressed with the epithet "indulgent?"

When we see judges, juries, ordinaries of Newgate, police magistrates, and other public functionaries, whose hearts are supposed to have become as the nether millstone through much practice,—whose eyes, as those of the lynx,—whose ears, as those of the mole,—taken in year after year by the protestations of malefactors, and petitioning the Home Office for reprobates capable of picking the turnkey's pocket of their reprieve, or biting off the ear of the ordinary who has recommended them to mercy, it is impossible to wonder at the unsophistication which exposes the less wary classes of the community to be quacked to death by plausible doctors, ruined in lawsuits by plausible solicitors, or won over to adoration by plausible moralists in prose and verse.

It is scarcely possible to be always on one's guard; and there is no mendicity society of good company established for the due examination of people's claims. If, in dread of imposition, we refuse our obolus to the real Belisarius, we never forgive ourselves; or if we reject with nausea some over-sweetened cup of sweets, the leprous distilment is poured into the porches of our ears as into those of *Hamlet's* father, some afternoon when we are napping, and our scruples are set at eternal rest!

There is a certain Jonathan Wilson, Esq., a man to whom the hats of bankers fly off in the streets,—whose name figures as director of half-a-dozen companies, and governor of half-a-dozen institutions. The bankers reverence the governors and directors; the companies and institutions reverence the man who commands the respect of bankers; and, while standing like a colossal Crœsus, with a foot upon the necks of each, Jonathan Wilson can afford to be not worth a guinea.

Jonathan Wilson was the younger son of a younger brother, without a shilling he could by birthright call his own. Air is sorry food for any thing but cameleons and orchidaceous plants;— more particularly to a man born like Jonathan Wilson, with an appetite for turtle and venison. After turning over in his mind the space to be measured between a dry crust and three courses and a dessert,—after examining, with a most curious eye, the turnpike roads which lead to the Temple of Fortune, such as industry, talent, and so forth, Jonathan decided upon attempting the by-path of Plausibility; and as coachmen diminish the steepness of a hill by a zigzag course, began to insinuate himself up the steep ascent by a serpentine career, bowing and smiling on either side, as the sinuosities of his pathway seemed to justify.

Jonathan was mild in his demeanour; gentle, patient, unpretending. Although he preached, because preaching was the order of the day, his homilies were couched in Chesterfieldian phrase. He never mentioned hell to ears polite; but persuaded the good that they had regenerated him; the bad, that they had corrupted; and both, that it was their business to take care of their own.

After being adopted as confidential man to every body having confidence, that is money to dispose of, with the money of the few he soon commanded the respect of the many; and has now a mansion in Portland Place, a villa at Tottenham, and more turtle and venison than he can devour. He has acted as churchwarden, he has officiated as sheriff—he might be in parliament if he chose. But, according to the argument of the Danish sailors, who would not send Hamlet into England, because "all the men there were as mad as he," Jonathan Wilson shirks an assemblage so eminently remarkable for its plausibility.

Has not this man speculated cunningly upon the gullibility of the world?—Yet Jonathan Wilson is a drop in the ocean of Plausible People.

The Chaperon and
the Debutante

I T IS A CURIOUS FACT, that almost all the by-words we have
borrowed from the French language, have ceased to be used in
a similar sense in their own country. The designation *débutante*,
for instance, is only applied in France to first appearances at the
theatre; and the word *chaperon* is nearly obsolete. In the higher
classes of Parisian society, unmarried girls are so rarely to be seen
(never, unless under the protection of a parent), that an occasion
seldom presents itself for the use of the terms chaperon and
débutante.

Among ourselves, meanwhile, they have become naturalized.
Among ourselves—where marriage, instead of being "dealt
with by attorneyship," and, consequently, placed within every
one's power of attainment, is, as well as entering a business or
a profession, the result of preference or caprice; young ladies
are introduced into society, in all the innocence of ringlets and
white muslin, as soon as they are able to distinguish a quadrille
from a polka—orgeat from lemonade; and, whereas, at the same
tender years, their youthful minds might not be equally skilled
to discriminate between the good match and the pitiful younger
brother,—the gentleman with serious intentions and the mere
ball-room flirt,—the "wisdom of our ancestors" provides them
with a female friend or relative as temporary guardian of their
person;—a full-dress governess, under whose turban is supposed
to reside as much knowledge as under the wig of the Lord

Chancellor, and under whose starched draperies is concentrated the discretion of a Mrs. Chapone.

In contemplating the soft, blushing, trembling, smiling Débutante tricked up from head to foot as though she had just stepped out of a *Journal des Modes*, ready to sink into the earth with confusion, under the gaze of the profane, we are tempted to exclaim with the poet:

> Was ever thing so pretty made to stand?

But a prosaic parody on the line suggests itself, the moment we turn towards her obligato accompaniment, the officious, lynx-eyed Chaperon, till we can scarcely resist murmuring

> Was ever thing so fussy made to stand—*still?*

One of the peculiar faculties of the experienced Chaperon is ubiquity. She is in all places at once; beside the refreshment table, in the card-room, watching the dancers; nay, retreat into the furthermost and most flirtiferous corner of the ball-room, with the Débutante leaning on your arm—behind a door, a screen, a curtain, a rose-tree—and, on looking up, you will find the piercing grey eyes of the Chaperon fixed inquiringly upon your manœuvres!

They penetrate, like Perkins's steam gun, through a six-inch iron plate; and, as to common deal, it becomes diaphanic as gauze, whenever the Chaperon approaches. Damask hangings are mere air when interposed between her and the object of her solicitude; and, like hunger, she can eat through a stone wall, if divided for nefarious purposes from her kitling. Parents and guardians, nurses, governesses, turnkeys, keepers, inspectors of police, are not to be compared, in point of vigilance, with the Argus-like zeal of an accomplished Chaperon.

The Chaperon is usually a spinster, having much leisure and little superfluity of coin; or a widow, without offspring of her own; or a matron, who, having married off her own daughters, is desirous to benefit the rising generation with the results of her experience. The mother, accompanying her children into society, and exercising her maternal solicitude in their behalf, does not come under the denomination of Chaperon. It is usually with interested views that the gratuitous office is undertaken.

The Débutante in want of a Chaperon, is often the daughter of a widower, to whom it is good to make apparent that so tender and valuable a protectress would be still tenderer and more valuable as a step-mother. In other instances, the office is assumed by the prudent spinster, having no equipage of her own, with a view of being franked to the various fetes for which she has secured invitations. By a spinster still further removed from the world's favour, the post of Chaperon to an attractive Débutante is actually sought as a letter of introduction to the pleasures of society.

Miss Clarissa Spyington, for instance, being well aware that the rich and lovely Helena Lennox will be invited to all the best balls of the season, prevails upon the young lady's guardian, her cousin, Sir Paul Spyington, the wealthy banker of Portland Place, to institute her as Chaperon to the heiress. In order to do honour to her office, she even stoops to assume brevet rank; and, thenceforward, prints herself upon her cards "Mrs. Spyington;"—a matronly designation that invites confidence, and repels raillery.

Sir Paul is certainly so far justified in his election, that the maiden lady, whether as Miss or Mistress, is admirably qualified for the discharge of her duties. Having simpered away the days of her own debutancy at Bath, so long ago that the memory of her charms has passed away with that of the beauship of Nash, or minuet of Tyson, she has since successively paraded the parades of all the watering-places in the three kingdoms. The pantiles could swear to the tread of her Spanish leather slipper. The Steyne prates of her whereabout. Cheltenham, Malvern, Leamington, Harrowgate, Weymouth, Ramsgate—nay, even the esplanade of Beulah Spa, have their tales to tell of the marchings and counter-marchings of the unfair Clarissa.

In the course of these transitions, Mrs. Spyington has necessarily picked up useful knowledge, "as pigeons peas." She has the peerage, baronetage, and even the voluminous records of Burke's

Landed Gentry at her fingers' ends; with all their family histories, genealogies, arms, and emblazonments. Let not, therefore, the partner aspiring to the hand of the charming Helena Lennox in the waltz, presume to give himself out as one of the "Heathcotes of Rutlandshire." Mrs. Spyington will detect his vain pretences; Mrs. Spyington will put him in his place. Before he had been twice in company with the Debutante, Mrs. Spyington managed to ascertain that he was only a young barrister, the son of "people in Baker Street;" people without a country seat, whom she remembered in cheap lodgings at Broad- stairs; people comprised under the comprehensive designation of "the Lord knows who."

It was not for such a man to be seen dancing a second time in the course of the evening with the heiress of the late Sir Hector Lennox, of Lennox Castle.

But it is not alone with the name and nature of the Débutante's partner she is conversant. The Chaperon is familiar with the birth, breeding, and history of every body, in every room she enters. Not a carriage drives along Portland Place, but, from the arms and livery, she can predicate concerning the names and fortunes of its owners, as a gipsy reads them in the lines of a hand that has been duly crossed with silver or gold. Nay, when at fault concerning the features of some consequential dowager, the Chaperon is able to identify her by her very diamonds.

"That must be the Dowager Marchioness of Methuselah; I remember her at Queen Charlotte's Drawing Rooms, in the early part of the present century, when I always had a Star Chamber ticket from a friend in the Board of Works. Lady Methuselah was then a very sweet woman. I have a perfect recollection of her in that very aigrette and bouquet, in a yellow crape hoop, looped up with white acacias and Roman pearls. It was just when there was the talk of an invasion. The Marchioness's charming daughters were at that time unmarried. Lady Maria is now the Duchess of Dunderhead; but Lady Harriet made a poor match—Lady Harriet, poor thing, is only Lady Harriet Titmouse. The Titmouse's have a fine estate in Essex, but they are no great things. Between ourselves, I have heard it whispered in their neighbourhood, that the grandfather of the present Titmouse was a Sheriff of London, citizen and cordwainer, or some dreadful thing of that description. But the Marchioness, of course, knows not a syllable of the matter. The Marchioness, like all those belonging to that venerable old court of Queen Charlotte, is exceedingly nice on such points. Any one may perceive with a glance that the Marchioness is a conservative. She has not varied so much as the set of her diamonds for the last fifty years. In these fantastical days, it is not so easy to identify a woman by her jewels. Reform, reform, reform, in every direction. And pray admire the result! All the beautiful old breastknots and stomachers, which were shamefully transformed into aigrettes, buckles, and broaches a few years ago, are actually being converted into stomachers again; for family diamonds are treated with as little reverence as a close borough or a sinecure. Ah! things would be very differently managed if we had a few more such women in the world as the Marchioness of Methuselah."

At first, the Débutante is charmed with the loquacity of her Chaperon, which serves as a cover to her timidity. By degrees, she learns to prize it on other accounts. While Mrs. Spyington gabbles on about the Marchioness, of whom she knows nothing, Miss Lennox is enabled to give her attention to the Mr. Heathcote of whom her Chaperon wishes her to know nothing; and who profits by the monologue of the lady in the turban, to place himself in Paradise close at the ear of Eve.

But it is not so easy to deceive the vigilance of the professional dragon. Though the Chaperon, like the "blind mole, he not a footfall," she has an intuitive sense of the approach of danger; and, even as a hen gathers her chickens under her wings long before the hovering hawk is perceptible to human eyes, Mrs. Spyington, though the son of the " people in Baker Street" is invisible, crooks her arm like the pinion of a well-trussed fowl, twitches off the Débutante into a less dangerous neighbourhood, and plants her on a bench of dowagers, unapproachable by anything short of the Duke of Wellington or the conqueror of the Hesperides.

Whenever a tender Débutante is seen thus guarded round with turbans, ruffs, ruffles, and India shawls, let it be understood that she is in limbo—in durance, not vile, but illustrious; a sort of honorary ward in Chancery; like the crown jewels in the Tower of London, seen by candlelight through a grating.

It is a curious branch of ball-room science to examine, step by step, the mental progress of the Débutante of another class—Miss Tibbs. At her first ball, her perceptions are vivid, her impulses natural. Enchanted to have escaped from the schoolroom, Mrs. Marcet's Rational conversations, Herz's exercises, roast mutton, and rice pudding,—to have exchanged jacconot or merino for silk or tulle, and the heavy morocco slipper for one of sandalled satin,—the first twang of Weippert's harp, as she enters the dancing room,

> Takes her imprison'd soul
> And laps it in Elysium.

The clustered lights of the chandeliers and girandoles dazzle her unpractised eyes; the glitter of jewels, the gleam of satins, the glow of flowers, excite the flutter of her girlish spirits. The very heart within her twitters as she hears her name announced, and sees a hundred admiring eyes directed towards her new dress:— with how different a pulsation, alas! from the tender anxieties she is likely to experience in re-entering the same scene six months afterwards.

Unless provided with a Chaperon of real and acknowledged merit, that is, of extensive connexions and persevering officiousness, the young lady, at her first *entrée*, trembles for her chance of a partner. What if all the pains bestowed upon her well-starched petticoat, her satin slip, and aërophane tunic, her transparent stocking, close-fitting shoe, and still closer-fitting glove (for to be *bien ganté* is beginning to be an article of ballroom religion in London, as it has always been in Paris); what if the anxious care bestowed by Monsieur Rigodon for the last ten years on her feet, and by Monsieur Isidore, for the last half-hour on her head, in order that the *bandeaux* of the one may be as exquisitely smooth as the *pas de bourrées* of the other, should end in her being fated to sit still all the evening, and write herself down "a bencher of the inner temple" of Terpsichore!

Agitated by these misgivings, she wonders to see her Chaperon take her place deliberately in the card-room, as though there were no such things as quadrilles and waltzes in the world,—as though people came to a ball to shuffle their cards instead of their feet. Thus placed, however, she commands a view of the dancing-room; and, by dint of edging forward her seat, (to the indignation of a corpulent gentle woman into whose knees she carelessly inserts the angular corner of the chair she is coaxing, edgeways, to the front rank), manages to place herself within view of the young gentlemen lounging up and down, in order to pass in review the belles of the evening. One or other of them, she fancies, cannot fail to be struck by the elegance of her costume and manners. Her great difficulty consists in preserving the downcast air, insisted upon by her Chaperon as indispensable to the character of a Débutante, and keeping sufficiently on the alert to ascertain whether anything eligible in the way of partnership is approaching.

During the first five minutes, she is convinced that every young gentleman in a white cravat, waistcoat, and kids, with varnished pumps and cobweb stockings, long straight hair, and short curled whiskers, who looks a second time at her, has "intentions." But alas! they pass and make no sign! "Another and another still succeeds;" the fiddles quavering, the violoncello grunting, the harp twanging, the flageolet squeaking invitingly all the time.—Still, alas ! no partner!

At length, one of those who had gazed most fixedly upon her charms (a slim adolescent, in a flashy waistcoat and black cravat, against whom, the moment she caught sight of him, she decided in the negative, as "a shocking style of man"), accosts the lady of the house; and, while directing her observation towards the corner where the halpless Débutante is ensconced, is evidently asking an introduction to "the lovely creature in white crape with pink roses."

The breath of the Débutante comes short! She is undecided what to do. He is certainly ill-calculated to make a figure in her journal. She fears he will not do to write about in her next letter to dear Matilda, at Brighton. Ten to one his name is Smith—

"JOHN SMITH!" or he may be an ensign in a marching regiment, or a banker's clerk, or a clergyman's younger son!

She has half a mind to decline dancing altogether. Yet it seems ill-natured to refuse a young man who means well, and has done nothing to offend her; and, after all, an indifferent partner is better than no partner at all. Moreover, when once seen figuring in an "*en avant deux*" she is sure of having crowds of eligibles at her feet.

On the whole, therefore, she thinks it better to be placable; and, as the lady of the house advances towards her, followed by the agitated youth, kneading in his hands the edges of his new silk hat by way of keeping himself in countenance, she looks the other way, and tries to appear as unconcerned as she can. Fancying that the eyes of the whole room are upon her, the elated Débutante trembles lest her perturbation should be too plainly visible through the folds of her lace tucker.

The lady of the house is now opposite, bending towards her, as well as a hard steel busk and a corset as rigid as a bench of Middlesex magistrates, will admit; till all the feathers of her satin hat are set nodding by the discomposure of her equilibrium. The Débutante meanwhile, feels her colour rising with contending emotions. But it rises still higher, when she hears her corpulent neighbour addressed by the lady of the house with, "Will you give me leave, my dear Mrs. Hobbleshaw, to present to you the only son of your old friend, Lady Pinchbeck? Sir Thomas is a stranger in town, and vastly desirous of the honour of your acquaintance." Whereupon the young gentleman in yellow kids bows awkwardly, and taking his station behind the chair of the corpulent gentlewoman, commences an interesting dialogue, and turns his back upon the Débutante for the remainder of the evening.

The poor girl is ready to cry with vexation. She would not have come to the ball, had she expected to be so treated! Nor does her irritation diminish when her Chaperon turns towards her, at the close of the third rubber, with the inquiry of "Miss Tibbs, my love, havn't you been dancing?—Dear me, how provoking!—It is all on account of your hiding yourself in that foolish corner.— Wouldn't you like to take some refreshment ?"

Cramped with sitting three hours and a half upon a cane-bottomed chair, the Débutante is right glad to hook herself to the Chaperon's arm, elbow her way into the refreshment-room, and, while waiting half an hour for her turn to approach the table, and feeling the roses of her trimming crushed flat as crown-pieces in the throng, she accepts the offer of some vanille ice, receives it over the head of a squat lady at the risk of dislodging it into her neighbour's turban or her own bosom; and, after soiling her gloves with a wet spoon, and getting her elbow jogged at every mouthful, to the imminent risk of her white satin slip, is anxious to crush her way back again into the dancing-room.

The Chaperon, however, is still diligently at work on an overflowing plate of lobster salad, to which tongue and chicken, or a slice of *galantine*, are likely to succeed. *She* has managed to obtain a snug berth for herself at the supper table; and is ensconced, with a glass of champagne at her right-hand, and a tumbler of sherry and water at her left, without any idea of giving in for twenty minutes to come.

The Chaperon has constitutionally, an untirable voracity. She is the shark of the female world. Like her prototype, the Dragon of Wantley, she is able to devour houses and steeples (of spun sugar and Savoy cake), and wash them down with an ocean of Roman punch. Throughout her six rubbers per night, she continues to imbibe, every ten minutes, glasses of negus in winter,—of ice in summer; solidified by basketsful of sponge-biscuits and maccaroons, which disappear as if thrown into a lime-kiln.

> Like affection's dream,
> They leave no trace behind.

The Débutante on the contrary, "scarcely confesses that her appetite is more to bread than stone." Like other humming-birds, she is nourished upon saccharine suction. It suffices for her to look once a day at a spoonful of minced veal; and, like the boa constrictor, to make a heavy meal once a month, on—the wing of a partridge. Unless accidentally detected at her private luncheon, the Débutante was never seen to eat!

At the close of the Chaperon's prolonged repast, feeling thoroughly restored, she observes aloud to her charge, "Well,—now that we have made ourselves quite comfortable again, I am sure, my dear, you would like to dance." The couple of sovereigns she has netted, incline her to return to the card-table; and as the Débutante, who is musing over the destruction of her ball-dress in the crowd, remains pensively silent, the Chaperon sidles up to their hostess, and executes a mysterious whisper, to which the weary lady in the hat and feathers, who has been courtseying for the last three hours and three quarters, with various signs of condescension, replies by an assenting nod.

The result of this diplomatic conference becomes apparent, when, five minutes afterwards, the lady brings up for judgment a genteel youth in nankeen pantaloons, an inch or two of whose meagre wrists are perceptible between the dress-coat he has outgrown and the overgrown gloves which wrinkle down over his thumbs; and whose straight, yellow hair is combed up, tent-wise, on the top of his head, like the brass flame with which the gas manufactories crown the ornamental bronze vases on their gate-posts; a shapeless booby, whose only care is not to giggle during the presentation.

"You *must* dance with him—it is her own nephew;" whispers the Chaperon, foreseeing the refusal of her charge; and with indignant soul, accordingly, poor Adeliza Tibbs deposits her fan and bouquet, and stands up, for the first time of her life, in the most insignificant corner of the most insignificant quadrille that has been danced in the course of the evening.

Nevertheless, the display, poor as it is, revives her spirits. She sees a tall, distinguished-looking young man, her *vis-à vis*, inquire her name; and decides that he intends to invite her for the next dance. She is sure he is meditating an introduction.

Previous, however, to the final *chassé croisé* of the odious set into which she has been betrayed, the Chaperon glides insidiously towards her with intelligence that "the carriage has been waiting for the last hour; that her papa is terribly particular about his horses; and that she faithfully promised Mr. Tibbs not to keep either his coachman or daughter out after two o'clock."

The boa and mantle, pendent upon her skinny arm, attest the firmness of her sinister intentions; and the poor Débutante, having no engagement to plead in opposition, is muffled up, and carried off in triumph. Not choosing to confide the mortifications of the evening to the attendant by whom she is disrobed, she is forced to pretend fatigue as the origin of her fallen countenance when her mangled ball-dress is held up to her commiseration, with an exclamation of "How you *must* have danced, Mem, to have been squeedged to pieces in this way!"

Three months afterwards, the Débutante even when not endowed with the weighty attractions of a Miss Helena Lennox, has, probably, contrived to recommend herself so far to the civilities of the dancing world, as to be sure of partners to her heart's content. The finest optical glass in Dollond's shop would not now enable her to discern the hapless youth in the nankeen continuations; although he contrives to cross her path fifty times at every ball, and obtrude as her *vis-à-vis* whenever she has the misfortune to undergo a partner not sufficiently adroit to provide one of her own selection.

The Débutante has now become fine, choice, exclusive. She has no further objection to the permanent establishment of her Chaperon in the card-room; having succeeded in persuading that august functionary that the crowd in the doorway often renders it impossible to rejoin her between the dances. She is engaged three deep, both for waltz and quadrille; and, lest she should be missed by her cavalier at the moment the dance is making up, contrives to be passed from partner to partner, throughout the evening, like an Irish vagabond handed from parish to parish, all the way from Dover to Holyhead.

You may see her smiling in succession upon the arm of every beau in the room. Majors, captains, lieutenants, cornets, ensigns; "the three black graces—law, physic, and divinity;" raw baronets, and hobble-de-hoy heirs-apparent, claim her successively as their own.

'T is "Si, Signor;"
'T is "Ja, mein herr;"
'T is "S'il vous plait, monsieur."

To all, and each, she utters the same emphasised fractions of common-place, broken up with a view to sweeten polite conversation. The room is shockingly hot, or dreadfully crowded. Strauss's last waltz is infinitely prettier than all the rest; or, she really wonders even the chairs can stand still, when Jullien is playing.

To fifteen partners an evening, does she show her teeth, her wit, and the point of her white satin Slipper. The captain, who has the misfortune to snap the encrusted sticks of her fan *à la Louis XIV.*, is now a horrid creature; "the major who procures her tickets for the rehearsal at the opera, a charming man." When hurried into her father's carriage at the close of four hours' incessant flirtation and salutation, the Débutante is as much elated with her conquests, real or imaginary, as the Chaperon with the game bagged in her card purse.

Three months after this, another change has come over the spirit of her dream. The major is *now* a "horrid creature;" and she will hear of nothing included in the pages of the army-list, under a G.C.B. She can recognise a younger brother by the sit of his coat, and prattles of "scorpions" and "detrimentals" like the worst of them; is shocked at the idea of labouring through a quadrille more than once or twice in the course of the evening; and is sure to be engaged for the two first waltzes before she enters the ball-room.

Instead of casting down her eyes, as at first exacted by her Chaperon, her enfranchised looks challenge every living soul around her; and the finical Adeliza has even mounted an eye-glass, through which, with a scornful smile, she scrutinises the Dison's lace of fat Mrs. Hobbleshaw. She has actually refused Sir Thomas Pinchbeck; and is suspected of a design upon the hand of the Honourable Henry Hottentot.

While the Débutante has been thus progressing in her accomplishments, the Chaperon has not been inactive. It is owing to her instructions that Miss Tibbs has acquired so precocious an insight into the mysteries of the peerage, and such accurate powers of detecting the "complement extern" of a younger brother. It is the Chaperon who has finessed for invitations for her; and spread advantageous rumours of the amount of her father's fortune; to which (sinking the claims of two brothers at Rugby, one at the Naval College, and another at Woolwich, all of whom the Chaperon elliptically passes over) she is nearly the heiress.

No numeration table is sufficiently comprehensive for the number of Miss Tibbs's suitors and refusals The Chaperon will not hear of her settling at present. Having serious intentions of accompanying her to Cheltenham for the autumn, and Brighton for the winter, she suggests that it would be a pitiful thing to accept a Sir Thomas Pinchbeck, a mere country baronet with a wretched two thousand a-year, who would not be able to afford her so much as a box at the opera. Her dear Adeliza's acquaintance is now so much extended, that there is no surmising what might be the result of "another season." The Chaperon has had a private hint of an Irish peer who is immensely struck, and going to Cheltenham, in the express hope of meeting the sweet girl to whom he lost his heart in a gipsy party at Beulah Spa.

The Débutante (who, thanks to the grandiloquence of her Chaperon concerning the ways and means of the house of Tibbs), has now nine obedient humble servants in the household brigade, to say nothing of lancers and light dragoons, an Irish member, and a saucy clerk in the Treasury is now beginning to think imperial Tokay of herself, and will not hear of derogation. She treats her Chaperon like a Turk; and comes and goes at the hours that suit her, without regard to the horses or the lady in the turban. She insists upon the footman serving her breakfast in gloves; will not take a glass of water from the hands of her maid, unless brought on a salver; talks politics with the Irish member; is of opinion that Sir Robert is the person to save the country; calls the dear Duke "our own Coriolanus;" and is about as silly and conceited a little Miss as any in her Majesty's dominions.

In a higher walk of life, the Débutante is a less specific personage. Lady Sophia (whose first appearance at Almack's, after her presentation at Court, places her in a scarcely more public position than she has been occupying, evening after evening, for four years previous, at the country-seat of her father, the earl) is a very different person from the blushing, fluttering, giggling

Miss Tibbs. All that the Débutante of the middle classes is left to discover from personal experience, *she* has learnt from the experience of others. In her very accidence, she was too knowing to mistake a younger for an elder son—a new knight for an old baronet; and as to showy officers, the whole army-list figures, in her imagination, as a set of nobodies, not worth a thought, till they attain the rank of field officers; the army being an *omnium gatherum*, into which fathers of families thrust their supernumerary sons, who are good for nothing else.

Lady Sophia does not vary her pretensions, or cast her nature twice-a-year, like the less illustrious Miss Adeliza Tibbs.

Blushes, God help you, she has none to loses Sir!

She was *born* self-possessed; and never knew what it was to be flurried by a partner or a declaration. Instead of humbly following in the wake of fashion, she heads the procession; invents flounces—introduces a new *capote*—is great at private theatricals assumes to herself, without apology, the part of Helen or Venus in a *tableau*—rattles through the *chansonnettes* of Levassor ; and all this with such perfect ease of high and pretence at decorum, that—

The holy priests bless her when she is riggish.

Lady Sophia has no fears concerning her settlement in life. The Duke of Belton and her father have long arranged an alliance between their respective children. But, even were she not tacitly affianced to the Marquis, one or other of her father's numerous nephews, or guests, or constituents, would be readily attracted by the merits of a damsel so well born, with a fortune of thirty thousand pounds. "The Morning Post," and "The Book of Beauty," taking care that her claims to distinction shall not be overlooked, she is as well advertised as Cox and Savory's hunting and Lady Sophia is one of those Débutantes who have no chance of degenerating into Chaperons, unless to daughters of their own.

Of Miss Tibbs, on the other hand, the destinies are less accurately defined by fate. Like all Débutantes who fall into the frailty of flirting; it is probable she will come in time to be opprobriated as a coquette, or shunned as a jilt. The roses will shed their leaves, and the thorns become apparent. The brothers at Rugby, Woolwich, and the Naval College, will grow up; and, accompanying her into society, supersede all false notions of her consequence, and the services of the superannuated Chaperon. The Mrs. Hobbleshaw, whom she has quizzed, and the Sir Thomas Pinchbeck, whom she has rejected, will seize upon this moment for revenge.

As years progress with the mortified damsel, they will preserve a perpetual memorandum of the date of her *début*; thanks to which, the world is privileged to discover that her bloom is less variable than of; her ringlets less liable to the effect of damp than when they were the native produce of her empty head.

New Débutantes will display their round fair forms in afflicting contrast with her bony rectangularity. She will be set aside like a last year's almanack, or obsolete edition.

The Chaperon, to whom the worthy Mr. Tibbs unites himself in his dotage in gratitude for her extreme care of his daughter and coach-horses,—will now recommend her to try a fresh line of business, and attempt a new *début* as a blue—or serious young lady—or political economist,—or something still more novel and original.

But Adeliza has grown weary of her vocation. A second *début*, she knows, is like a second attack of small-pox —invariably fatal; and stranger things have happened than her taking refuge from the ignominy of spinsterhood, under the wing of the quondam young gentleman of the nankeens, now a thriving country banker in drab shorts and mahogany tops; whose yellow crest has given way to a sober baldness, highly becoming the position of a man well-to do in the world.

It would have been a bold attempt, however, to hazard a prediction of such a termination to her career, when she first blushed her way into society under the care of her CHAPERON, as an aspiring DÉBUTANTE.

The Cabinet Ministress

C<small>ABINET</small> M<small>INISTERS</small> <small>HAVE</small> <small>BEEN</small> <small>OFTEN</small> and ably portrayed, both by themselves and others. But there is one portion of the Cabinet Minister—*i.e.*, his better-half—that still remains to be delineated; an anomalous individual, to whom the nation supplies a local habitation, and for whom, henceforward, we shall supply a name. For there is no more reason why Ambassador should have its feminine in the vernacular, than Minister; and we propose hence forward to follow the example of the Germans, in whose provincial towns you may hear announced, "Mrs. Deputy Sub-Inspectress of the Royal and Imperial Mines and Forests;" or "Mrs. Upper-Land-Stewardess of the Parochial District of so-and-so."

The Cabinet Ministress is, in our opinion, an ill-used person, considering the large portion of the business of the State gratuitously harnessed upon her fair shoulders. The Cabinet Ministress is, in fact, the great unpaid—*sans* salary, *sans* perquisites, *sans* patronage, *sans* everything;—yet expected to be the obedient humble servant of the throne and the public every hour of the day—every day in the year, from eight o'clock in the morning till six the morning following, from the 1st of January to the 31st of December.

The Cabinet Ministress has no quarter, and no quarter-day. She works like a slave; and, if refractory, is reminded, like other slaves, that the hour of emancipation will be the hour of her ruin;

that it is Lombard Street to a China orange; that she must either be the Cabinet Ministress and a drudge, or plain Lady Titmouse and a nobody.

We might have hesitated to draw public attention towards a character apparently of a private nature, were it not that our present Premier and his predecessor are widowers.[1] No personality can be imputed. The kind-hearted being who should be now enjoying the honours and exercising the labours of Premièreship, is at rest. "After life's fitful fever she sleeps well;" and the female history of Downing Street, for once, presents a blank.

The interregnum is, at least, favourable to the delineation of the unnatural task-work,

> grief, and pain,
> That has been, and may be again.

In the first place, the Cabinet Ministress has to endure, *par ricochet*, all the ill-humour of the throne. Whenever the Premier has shown himself stubborn with the King his master, concerning a new war, new tax, new favourite, new antipathy,—concerning secret supplies or public animosities suggested by the voice of royalty, (not the less absolute for being still and small),—the queen-consort thinks it necessary to mark her resentment to the Premiere.

It is amazing in how many modes this may be effected. The French have taught us three hundred and sixty-five ways to dress eggs. The number of fashions in which sovereignty can trick up its displeasures is more than double! It speaks volumes in a single glance, and libraries in a courtesy; or, by omitting either, can "Kill, kill, kill, kill," as ruthlessly as Lear. When the Cabinet Ministress makes her appearance at Court to perform her official ko-too, the aspect of royalty is watched by all present, to ascertain the temperature of her welcome; and, according as that august countenance freezes or thaws, those of the titled mob, are bright or sinister. The stability of the administration is opined upon, according to the indications of the barometer of that variable atmosphere, the breath of Kings.

The Cabinet Ministress is invited to share the bread and salt of the royal table; and those who know not what duplicity is in Courts, predict that all must be safe; or she is coldly looked upon, and not a civil syllable is uttered of inquiry after her sick children or gouty father; and people go and sell out of the stocks, not dreaming how many masks are assumed to lead astray the surmises of political antagonism.

Another of the *peines fortes et dures* sustained by Cabinet Ministresses, is that of doing the honours of the country to illustrious foreigners, not quite grand enough to be inmates of the palace, and too grand to be the guests of the commonalty.

These great unknowns, usually speaking no language but their own, must be chaperoned to St. Paul's, the Abbey, the Tower, like other country cousins; they must be escorted to the Opera, accompanied to Almacks, presented at Court. No matter whether the august visitor, flung with other burthens on the shoulders of the Foreign Office, be the Duchess of Hesse Holburg Fiddelhausen, or Quam Sham Heblez Fudgeroo, Princess Royal of the Sandwich Islands, Lady Downing Street must take care that her Royal or Serene Highness's sauerkraut, or sandwich of raw veal, is suitably adjusted; that her Royal or Serene Highness's court plume, or jacket of peacock's feathers, come home in due time from the plumassier; and should her Royal or Serene Highness be summoned to Bow Street, for fustigating her maids of honour, or carbonadoing a child for luncheon, the Cabinet Ministress is required to explain to her that she is in the wrong box, and that nothing enormous can be done in England without "an order from the magistrates."

The Cabinet-Ministress must possess a half-horse, half-alligator constitution. She must be ready to rattle in twenty minutes to Windsor—hail, rain, or shine,—whether on the eve of her confinement, or just recovering from the same,—whenever honoured with a summons to eat a slice of the royal venison, or take up a stitch in the royal *soutache*. She must be insensible to the perils and dangers of damp beds or smoky chimneys, when following the Court; and, should the Pavilion be the favourite toy of the reign, must on no account find the searching air of

Brighton too keen. Its rough visiting, like that of custom-house officers on landing from France, is a sacrifice due to the interests of Government.

Her appetite must be as sturdy as her limbs. However squeamish by nature, she must be ready to swallow turtle and venison *à discrétion*, whenever invited to figure at public dinners. "The Cabinet Ministers and their ladies" are required to be in readiness whenever the City of London feasts the City of Westminster, cramming its aldermen and custards down the throats of the dainty dames of May Fair. Wherever new bridges, railroads, or docks are opened to the public, hundred-and-twenty gun ships launched, statues inaugurated, or other grand national events solemnized with eating and drinking, the Cabinet Ministress must hob and nob with the local authorities, in order to have it supposed by the rest of the world that Government has had a finger in the pie.

If a tall showy woman, doing honour to her vocation, ten to one but the Cabinet Ministress will be asked to lay the first stone of a church, bridge, arch, college, lunatic asylum, or other national monument,—or to christen the ship with a bottle of pale sherry,—or hazard her life by being the first to skim along the new railroad, or by supporting, for three consecutive hours, the weighty politeness of the Lord Mayor.

But all this she must endure with smiling amenity. Whatever solemnities may take place during her husband's administration—whether the thermometer be three degrees below freezing point, or at ninety-two in the shade,—she must be able to stand half-a-dozen hours on a chilly pavement without a sneeze, or in the broiling sunshine without fainting or a *coup de soleil*. A parasol, fleecy hosiery, and the inborn strength of a Cabinet Ministress, will get her through her miseries. A bilious fever, caught at the Mansion House, would be an insult to the chief magistrate of the City of London; and, were she to complain of a fit of the rheumatism, as the result of some royal funeral or banquet in a barge, the attention of Parliament might, perhaps, be called to her delinquency by some factious Opposition Member.

But it is not alone to the festivals of the Home Department poor Lady Downing Street is required to do justice. Besides eating slices of a raw baron of beef in the Egyptian Hall, or an unctuous matelotte of eels, that look like segments of a boa constrictor, swan-hopping at Eel-pie island, the Cabinet Ministress is expected to assist in the celebration of all the birthdays of all the sovereigns in Europe—from the youthful Queen of the Peninsula, to the undying one, the veteran King of Sweden. She must not only have the almanack of Saxe Gotha at her fingers' ends, but be prepared to munch her way through it, as a promising child eats through its gingerbread alphabet. She must imbibe furlongs of maccaroni with the Ambassador of the Two Sicilies on the 12th of January; and swallow six ounces of caviar without wincing, with their Muscovite Excellencies on the 6th of July; nay, now that all Mussulman prejudices are abolished, it is probable that she may here after have to pull a pillau to pieces with her fingers at the Ottoman Embassy, or sup on "treacle, green figs, and garlic," with the representative of the Nawaub of Oude.

All this is very well, (*i.e.*, if it do not make her very ill) for these are duties of routine common to her predecessors, destined to her successors, and to be learned by questioning the very stones of the pavement of Downing Street. The grand difficulty of her vocation consists in a case of emergency; such as when the wife of the abdicated editor of the *Comet* or *Times*, or some other "leading journal which has lent its powerful aid to Government," is to be presented at Court, and the Cabinet Ministresses begin to shift the disagreeable duty from one to another. Or when there is a split in the royal family, and those favoured by the King are expected to be ungracious to the Queen; or those petted by the Queen required to be disrespectful towards some other members of the royal family. Nothing so difficult as to hit the exact medium due to the exigencies of royal taskmasters or mistresses. There must not be a scruple too much of bitterness or conscience, lest party newspapers take up the defence of the injured party. If the Sovereign turn his or her back upon certain individuals, the Cabinet Minister or Ministress may just glance at them over one shoulder. If the Sovereign refuse them an audience, the

Cabinet Minister or Ministress, must receive them standing. But if the Sovereign expressly direct that their memorials, letters, or other molestations, be left unanswered, the Cabinet Minister or Ministress may ignore their existence altogether for the remainder of their natural lives.

All this, and a great deal more, is duly impressed upon the mind of the Cabinet Ministress, from the moment her husband takes office. She is taught her lesson, as a bulfinch is taught to pipe; and nothing can be more curious than the occasional breaking forth of her natural notes, when her little official song escapes her memory or the skill with which she falls back again into "Marlbrook," or the "Duke of York's March," when she finds herself growing too natural. Her voice has a tone in talking about Ireland, the Corn-Laws, and other delicate questions, which could only have been instilled by a bird fancier.

Cabinet Ministresses, like captains, are casual things. The virulence of certain Tory Countesses, whenever they have an opportunity of giving tongue, is a proof how irritating are the effects of a fall from their high official estate, which, like other perils, leaves them, if not with broken bones, at least floundering in the mud.

We all know what a foolish-looking thing was the gilt grasshopper—to which we had looked up with reverence so long as it glittered at the top of the Royal Exchange,—when, brought down to the level of the earth, it lay, with other rubbish, in a tinman's yard. So is it with the Cabinet Ministresses, who, during the ascendancy of their party, were painted by the presidents of the Royal Academy; engraved by Doo, or Cousins; made frontispieces to annuals; sung by the Countess of Blessington, or some other fashionable laureate; and humbly implored to give their names and subscriptions to all the new works, all the new charities, all the new institutions,—to patronize charity balls or breakfasts in favour of asylums for every disease having a bustling Esculapius to maintain its importance, and be maintained by it in return;—to attest the virtues of the American soothing syrup, and the interesting object of "a case of extreme distress," at the risk of having a vote of censure passed upon their credulity by the College of Physicians, and the Mendicity Society.

After enjoying all this onerous popularity,—after being invited for the holidays to the best villas, and made to sink under a weight of tokens of fashionable regard,—the wresting the seals of office from the hands of their lords and masters, (or slaves) has sealed their destiny—They have become nothing, and *ex nihilo nihil fit.*—People who used to besiege their doors with visits, send cards of condolence by their footmen; and, the following season, forget to send them at all.

If they have formerly figured as beauties, the fickle voice of fashion now proclaims that they are "pretty, certainly, but silly, and vacant looking;" or if, when in office, applauded as wits, they are now discovered to be "ugly beyond permission," or "peevish as a sick parrot." From the day of vacating their place in Downing Street, their feet and hands grow large, their eyes and understandings small; and, both figuratively and materially, they lose a cubit of their stature.

And of all these miseries, the Cabinet Ministress is kept in hourly apprehension by the threats of the Opposition journals, and the utter dependence of her Spouse upon the breath of Kings, and buffetings of Parliament!—Like the senior captain of a marching regiment, she lives only in the hope of "getting the majority." At the political rubber, she remembers only the cards that are out, and trembles for the odd trick which is to secure her game. To her, life is a speculation. There are always odds for, or against her being something or nothing, that day six months; and, as a Cabinet Ministress is sure to have a host of indigent nephews or cousins to provide for, she grows feverishly anxious concerning divisions and adjournments.

While protesting that she is sick to death of the cares of place, and that all she wants is to get down to her country seat, instead of being fogged into an ague in London in the month of November, (when nothing is open in town but the patent theatres, and catacombs of the national cemetery,) she is, in fact, trembling lest she should have to pack her traps and be off.

If turned out, she knows that, like other ejected animals, she shall receive a kick from every one at parting; or, if required to bid "farewell, a long farewell to all her greatness," by the demise of her right honourable lord, feels that she shall be required to eat thrice as much dirt as other dowagers;—that the country will always be flinging in her teeth the pension which is to enable her to put something between them;—and, should she incline to second wedlock, let her remember the abuse heaped on Mrs. Perceval, and tremble!—Even though knocked off her pedestal, she must evermore deport herself as if still figuring thereon.

Such are the trying destinies of the Cabinet Ministress.

1. Written in the late reign, during the administration of Lord Melbourne.

The Linkman

WE ARE TOLD THAT THERE is but a step from the sublime to the ridiculous. It may be observed, with equal truth, that between the mobs of the great world and the swell mob there is only a LINK! A Linkman is, *bona fide*, the beggar defined by Hamlet, as "galling the courtier's kibe;"—a moral parody on the lady's page of the days of chivalry;—in spite of his rags, the only favoured mortal permitted to approach so near the Lady Dulcibella as she steps into her carriage after a ball, that his begrimed face and tattered garments are fanned by the fragrant breath and oriental perfumes of the court-beauty.

Like the heralds of old, the Linkman is a privileged person. Nay, he enjoys higher privileges than even the herald, whose office consisted in bearing the words of others, while the Linkman is allowed to give utterance to sentiments wholly his own. A court-jester or my Lord Mayor's fool is scarcely more sanctioned in the freedom of speech which tramples on all distinctions of rank and station, than the professional Link.

The Linkman may, in fact, be considered the public orator of the kennel. His knowledge of the men and manners that be, amounts almost to omniscience; and, saving Lord Brougham, there scarcely exists a man, in private or official life, who excels him in the manly frankness of telling people truths to their faces.

Not a dandy of Crockford's,—not a dowager of Grosvenor Square—whose name is not familiar in the mouth of the

Linkman as household words;—so much so, that he uses them as cavalierly as his goods and chattels, by superadding cognomens more appropriate than acceptable to the owners. Posterity might obtain considerable insight into the characters of many whom the Herald's Office styles "illustrious," and history is preparing to call "great," were it to employ reporters to stenograph, during a single evening, the ex-official debates among the henchmen of the flambeau at the door of the House of Commons, the Opera, and Almacks. The Linkmen of the day, or night, would throw considerable light upon the subject.

Unlike other popular representatives, the Linkman sees with unbiased eyes, and declaims with unblushing enunciation. The Linkman is never inaudible in the gallery. He is not only initiated into the secrets of the prison-house per privilege of place, as auditor of the last few words drawled between the Premier and the Home Secretary, as they separate at the door of their parliamentary den; or the few last whispers interchanged between the young Duchess and the idol of her soul, as he hands her into her chariot, after a third waltz at some fête in Berkeley Square; but he has not the slightest motive for rounding their periods or qualifying their expressions, after the fashion of the chartered fabricators of parliamentary eloquence or fashionable intelligence. The Linkman nothing extenuates, and sets down nought in malice.

"The old chap told the Mark is that for all his palaver, the Irish question was all my eye!"—is *his* literal interpretation of a ministerial colloquy;—and "The Capp'n swore to my lady as 'ow her eyes 'ad pitched it into 'im strong,"—is his equally faithful transcript of a declaration of love couched in the flowery generalities of Lalla Rookh or the Life Guards. The Linkman is consequently an accusing angel, who inscribes in his black book all the aristocratic indiscretions of the season.

What a singular destiny!—A very slight stretch of imagination might transform the ragged caitiff stationed with his link at the gates of some lordly palace, into a Spirit stationed with his flaming sword at the gates of Paradise! Celestial odours exhale upon him from those open portals. The music of a heavenly choir resounds in faint echoes from the distance. Emanations of ambrosial food deride his lips. He hears the flageolet of Collinet,—he savours the garnished chickens of Gunter,—he beholds the tripsome feet of Lady Wilhelmine or Lady Clementina flit by him;—and lo! he returns to the gnawing of his mutton bone and the twanging of his Jew's harp,—mocked by a Barmecide's feast of the imagination.

So far, however, from complaining of his destinies, he feels that it is something to have enjoyed even this " bare imagination of a feast;"—something to have fed on the crumbs falling from the table of beauty;—something to have been sanctified by a touch from the hem of the garments of those superhuman creatures. His brethren of the puddle are divided by a vast abyss from such angelic company. It is only the filthy torch he carries in his hand that entitles him to accost the shrinking beauty with, "Take your time, my lady!—please to take your time!—Only your ladyship's poor linkman! Rainy night, my lady; may I ask the servant for sixpence?"—so disposing his link during his apostrophe, that he is enabled to decide whether my lady's silken hose are laced or plain ; and whether her ladyship's white slippers be of silk or satin!—Not one of her adorers have approached her more familiarly in the course of the evening, than "her ladyship's poor linkman!"

It is astonishing the tact evinced by these fellows in ferreting out everything in the shape of an entertainment, from Pimlico to Whitechapel. Provided half a dozen carriages and hack cabs be gathered together, thither crowd the linkmen;—varying their apostrophes from "Take your time, my lady," to "Take your time, Mrs. Smith!" or "Shall I call up your lordship's people?" to "Please to want a cab, Sir?"

At the more brilliant balls, they are as inevitable as the *cornet à piston* of Koenig! One knows them like the cuckoo, by "their most sweet voices," rather than by their outward presentment, albeit revealed to view by the flaring of their links, as the ugliness of the imps of darkness in Don Juan, by the flashing of their torches.

These "winged voices," these connect

Airy tongues that syllable men's names,

themselves as intimately with the gaieties of Almacks' as if the Linkman held his patent of office from the Patroness's Bench. There is a peculiar hoarseness in their accents, as if the larynx, harassed by an eternal calling of carriages, had imbibed some mysterious distemper. They speak as through a speaking or like Demosthenes, trying to out roar the surges of the chafing ocean!

Much discussion has arisen of late years concerning the origin of the slang phrases of the day; and marvellous, indeed, is the universality of these axioms of street eloquence. But a common place cannot always have been a common place; and to *originate* a common place, is an effort of creative genius. The first man who said, "Does your mother know you're out?" uttered that which has been repeated by an enlightened population of at least a million of souls. If not witty himself, he has been the cause of wit in others, by inducing many an apt appropriation of a platitude.

Some assert that these cant words and slang phrases have their origin in the police reports; others that they spring to light and life in the galleries of the minor theatres. The truth is, that they are the legitimate and indisputable offspring of the Linkmen of the West End! Ask the policemen. Inquire of the standard footmen,—and they will inform you, that the first time they were ever pestered with interrogations concerning their mamma's mangle and pianoforte was by the Linkmen attending some fashionable assembly.

A few minutes' attention to their notes explanatory and commentatorial upon the carriages, as they successively drive up to a door, would suffice to prove their humour worthy the illustration of Cruikshank or Leech. A few years ago, when the Church, if not in danger, was in disgrace with the street orators of the metropolis, it was a favourite jest with the Linkmen to go bawling round the Opera House, in the thick of the crush of carriages after the opera, every Sunday morning,—The Archbishop of Canterbury's carriage!"—"The Bishop of London's carriage stops the way!"—"The Bishop of Exeter coming out!"— thereby impressing the multitude with a firm conviction of the levity, if not demoralization, of those eminent prelates. At the time of the Reform Bill, their vocabilities had a still more personal tendency; and to this day, all the biting truths inflicted upon the French ministers by the Charivari, are lavished *viva voce* on our English legislators, by the sarcasms of the linkboys.

In former times, before London was paved and lighted as becomes a civilized metropolis, every footman was his own linkman. The lackeys clustered behind a nobleman's carriage, or escorting a lady's sedan, carried each his torch, like pages on the stage in the old plays. Beside the entrance of many of the old-fashioned mansions in London may still be seen appended a huge iron funnel for extinguishing the flambeau or link.

But since the introduction of gas, the Linkman's "occupation's gone," as regards the livery of London. The flambeau is in desuetude; the link has retrograded to St. Giles's; nay, it now simply constitutes a badge to distinguish from the common herd the privileged callers-up of carriages. The noisy, officious, troublesome, roaring, boring rapscallions, who visit the pavement wherever a goodly mansion is lighted up for the reception of company, would be severally consigned to the station-house and Penitentiary as disturbers of the public peace, did they not bear in their hands an ensign of impunity. As the herald was protected by his wand—as the Chancellor by his mace—as the Archbishop by his crosier—as Majesty itself is dignified by the sceptre,—the interjectional portion of the mobility who call the coaches of the nobility, are by their links;—thereby entitled to vex the dull ear of night with their

Linked sweetness long drawn out.

The Linkmen of London are usually natives of the sister island,—which implies that they are poor, lean, hungerly, brisk, and knowing;—*Pat* at giving or taking offence. A jest-book might be concocted from their well-known repartees; and a series of romances compiled from the inedited memoirs of these enlightening members of society. Dodsley the man of letters, began life as a footman. I dare not say how high certain of our contemporaries have risen, who commenced as linkboys.—Let a single instance suffice.

Some five-and-thirty years ago,

In my hot youth, when George the Third was king,

there came, among other specimens of Irish starvation, from the Cove of Cork, the skeleton of a dapper-limbed young fellow, who, after fighting the king of terrors in the guise of typhus fever, famine, and Ballinasloe fair, had a mind to see whether the living which he found it impossible to pick up on Irish ground, were to be found, on any terms, in the kingdom of Cockaigne.

While bog-trotting and turf-cutting in his hungry boyhood, he had heard wondrous fairy tales of the city whose streets are paved with gold, whose houses are tiled with pancakes, and whose geese fly about ready stuffed, cackling for the spit and dying to be roasted; and was exceedingly disappointed when he arrived by long sea in the river, with a cargo of Irish butter, Irish pork, and Irish labourers, to find that people must work for their living in London, as elsewhere; but that work was not always to be had.

With a heavy heart did the new-corner seat himself on the stones of old London Bridge. In the desolation of his soul, he wept bitterly. He had not where to lay his head that night; and but for the opportune suggestion of some better impulse, such as that which instigated Whittington to "turn again" from the milestone, and aspire to the civic chair of London, Corney Cregan would perhaps have sought rest in the bed of the river that ran below. Hope whispered to him that in a capital glittering with such myriads of lights, and rumbling with such thousands of equipages, a brighter fate must be in store for him than amid the toiling moiling drudgery of his own poor gloomy native land.

Even the ardent temperament of an Irishman, however, all but gave way under the influence of a week's starvation and a week's mockery,—the isolation of an alien in a land of strangers!—The skeleton became still more gaunt, and its brilliant eyes burnt brighter in their sockets, under the excitement of want and desperation. From his youth upward, nothing had ever prospered with Corney. The cherry-trees from which he had been posted to drive away the birds, were sure to be more pecked than other cherry-trees. The field he was employed to sow, produced the scantiest crops; the hay he was employed to mow, was never known to dry.

And now, the same evil destiny seemed to pursue him in his new settlement! If he asked for employment, his shabby appearance was scouted; if he asked for charity, he was rebuked as too well dressed for a beggar; nay, when he attempted to pour his tale of woe into the ears of "the humane, whom Heaven hath blessed with affluence," as the advertisements have it, the richness of his brogue had so powerful an effect upon his auditors, that they were sure to wipe from their eyes tears arising from laughter rather than from emotions of sympathy.

Poor Corney's heart was ready to break. All this was worse than starving in Ireland. In Ireland people are used to starve, till like the eels, they think nothing of it!

But to starve in goodly streets abounding in cooks' shops, amid men and women who looked as if fed to compete for Smithfield prizes, was a realization of the pains of Tantalus! As he passed by the areas of the fashionable squares, and imbibed the aroma of stews and ragoûts issuing from the offices, it was not wonderful that he should conceive some mistrust concerning the text which talks of "filling the hungry with good things, and sending the rich empty away."

One summer afternoon, about the time when London sends forth its brightest equipages, adorned with the brightest human faces, to disport in the brightest sunshine of Hyde Park, poor Corney tottered his way from the miserable cellar in St. Giles's where he rented a bed at the price of two-pence a night and the succeeding day's worth of rheumatism, towards the fashionable quarter of the town,—leaning against the railings, the better to support his exhausted frame, and feeling that, if hunger could eat through stone walls, it was a shame that Providence sent him only brick ones to devour.

The strong man was now a weakling,—the cheerful one a misanthrope. Vainly had he addressed himself to the fair inmates of more than one showy carriage for the sorry dole of a halfpenny.

Though something in the picturesque wildness of his appearance for a moment captivated their attention, no sooner did his extended hand convince them that he was in need of charity, than they became shocked and frightened—muttered something about "wild Irishman," or "horrid Irishman,"—and desired the laced footmen in attendance to drive him away.

"Sorrow take 'em then, for hearts as black as the faces iv 'em is fair!"—was the only ejaculation of poor Corney as he turned doggedly away; and lo! when he applied in the same pitiful terms to passers by of his own sex, he found himself threatened with the Mendicity Society, or affronted by mention of a constable. If the poor man had only had strength to be indignant, he would have fired up at the insults put upon his country in his person.

Sauntering onward and onward, with a vague hope, proceeding from the increasing purity of the atmosphere, that he should reach green fields and blue skies at last, Corney traversed the brilliant tumults of Bond Street, crossed Berkeley Square, and at length took refuge on the doorstep of a handsome house in a street somewhat more secluded than the rest.

Though it was Seamore Place, poor Corney Cregan knew not that only a row of houses divided him from the pleasant pastures of Hyde Park. Resting his head upon his hands to relieve the dizziness arising from weakness and want, he began to indulge in visions of a brighter kind; soothing his pangs in England by hopes of heaven,—just as in old Ireland he had assuaged them by hopes of England, prosperity, and peace. In the extremity of his woe, he still pursued the instincts of a sanguine nature, and looked forward.

He was roused from his reverie by the approach of a horse entering the quiet street. All Irishmen are born with a weakness for horseflesh. Miserable as he was, he could not look without a feeling of satisfaction at the fine animal and its handsome young rider, so well-fitted for each others who appeared before him,

> A stately apparition sent
> To be a moment's ornament,

to the barren waste of his prospects. Starting up, poor Corney
fixed his eyes upon them with such beaming and undisguised
admiration, that something of the poetry of enthusiasm imparting
itself to his gaunt person, attracted in its turn the notice of the
young equestrian.

He was in the act of dismounting to pay a visit in the very
house upon whose door step Corney had been resting.

Can I trust you to hold my horse? said he, addressing the
poor fellow; who forthwith uttered in such uncouth accents his
promise to have a care of the "baste as though't were his own,"
as might have intimidated a less confiding nature, lest he should
so far treat it as his own as to ride off with it, and be heard of no
more.

The young man, however, who was also a young gentleman,
and an officer in the Life Guards, possessed a sufficient insight
into the mysteries of human physiognomy to intrust his property
to the hands of Corney Cregan. After a word or two of instruction
as to the mouth of the horse and the mode of holding the bridle,
Captain Wrottesley entered the house, after declining the civil
offer of one of the servants by whom the door was opened to
officiate as his groom during his visit.

The first ten minutes were very long to Corney; for his mind
was intent upon the few pence which he expected as the guerdon
of his office. But by the time a quarter of an hour had elapsed,
he was beginning to feel an interest in the fine animal under his
charge; and when, at the close of an hour, Captain Wrottesley
reappeared, his poor heart was actually cheered by such intimate
companionship with a beast so much more cared for, and so
much better fed than himself.

The young soldier, on the other hand, was pleased to find that,
instead of his horse being harassed, as is so often the case when
intrusted to the care of some casual guardian, his orders had been
strictly attended to. His visit had been a delightful one. His own
spirit was as much the lighter for it, as Corney's; so that, instead
of the shilling wherewith it was his custom to repay an hour's
attendance, he be stowed a whole half-crown upon his tattered
esquire.

Little did he suspect the opulence contained in that single coin, to the imagination of Corney Cregan! Within another hour, he had appeased the gnawing pangs of hunger, and taken out of pawn the jacket which had obtained him a shilling to keep him from starving the preceding week. That night, he slept like an Emperor!

The following day, about the same hour, but more from the desire to renew an agreeable reminiscence than from any expectation of encountering his benefactor again, Corney rambled to the same spot. Judge of his delight—when,—as he entered the secluded street, he saw the "iligant baste of a chisnut horse, and his darlin' of a rider," entering it at the further extremity and to his utter amazement, found his services again in request. The handsome young officer and his Bucephalus seemed expressly sent by Providence as a blessing upon poor Corney!—

"Harkye, my good fellow!" said Captain Wrottesley, at the close of his second visit, "you seem to be out of work, and living hereabouts. If you choose to try your luck every day at this hour, most likely I shall find you employment. I can't afford to give you half-crowns every day. A shilling is my stint for such jobs, and a shilling you shall have. Be here to-morrow. So long as I find I can rely upon you, you may rely upon me."

No need to record the countless benedictions lavished by poor Corney in the exuberance of his gratitude, upon Providence, the young officer, and the chesnut horse! It was as much as he could do to preserve a decent sobriety of deportment on his way home to St. Giles's; and when a week's official life had enabled him to lay by a sufficient sum, he felt it due to Captain Wrottesley to change his sleeping quarters to a mews in May Fair, in order to realize his patron's opinion that he was a denizen of the neighbourhood of Seamore Place.

It so happened that the daily visits which brought so bright a flush to the cheeks of the young guardsman, and imparted such brilliant vivacity to his eyes, were addressed to one with whose servants he was not willing to place his own groom in communication. It suited him to ride thither unattended; and it was consequently satisfactory to him to have secured a trustworthy fellow to take charge of his favourite horse during the happy lapse of time he was devoting to one still dearer to his affections.

Week after week, were the services of Corney retained. Already, he was becoming attached to his employer. There was something so fascinating in the open countenance of young Wrottesley, that Cregan would willingly have served him for nothing, had it been needful.

But the captain seemed to take as much pleasure in paying, as the poor Irishman in being paid. The shilling thrown to Corney was but a trifling token of the joy thrilling in the young man's heart as he issued from those doors, in peace and charity with all the world,—grateful to the enchanting friend he had left,—grateful to the sun for shining on him,—grateful to the noble horse he was about to ride,—grateful even to the poor ragged fellow who had taken such good care of it during his absence.

By degrees, the ragged henchman assumed a more respectable appearance. In a ticket-porter's scarlet waistcoat and sleeves, he tried to appear more deserving the service of him who risked his property in his hands. Wrottesley, on the other hand, took pride in his protégé's well-doing. In the course of three months' daily intercommunication, he had become so much interested in Corney's prospects, and so much touched by the gratitude of the warm-hearted fellow, as to recommend his services to his brother officers.

Thenceforward, Corney became the messenger of the Guards, as Mercury of the gods and, as a quaint mythologist has asserted that Hermes is represented with wings to his cap, as a token that the hat of a lackey ought to fly off to all mankind, the Irish peasant became courteous and humble in proportion as he rose in the world.

He was applauded for his civility almost as much as for his probity and address. Corney Cregan was pronounced to be a fellow whom anybody might trust with anything, and who might be trusted to deliver anything to anybody. He could not give offence. All the morning he held horses at the door of Captain Wrottesley's club, or went confidential errands, or carried parcels of trust;—at once the lightest light porter in St. James's Street, and the lightest hearted fellow in Great Britain!

As Corney became a man of substance, following the adage that "it is a poor heart that never rejoices," he allowed himself a little pleasure in addition to his multiplicity of toils. Addicted to theatrical amusements, he often favoured himself with a half-price entrance into the gallery, which enables a certain portion of the public to enjoy a view and hearing of the play, such as might be enjoyed out of a balloon. But if it scarcely enabled Corney to obtain much insight into what was passing on the stage, it introduced him to the acquaintance, at the doors of the theatre, of that worshipful confraternity, the Linkocracy of the London world. They were his countrymen, although he knew them not; and, after a due process of eating and drinking, swearing and singing, in their society, Corney Cregan was eventually induced to enlist in their regiment.—He purchased his first link, and became one of the Illuminati of the western world!

On this occasion, the high patronage enjoyed by the poor Irishman proved of material service to him. The first time Corney officiated at Almacks', he obtained so much custom from his old patrons, and such civil notice from old Townsend, to whom they recommended him, that he was accounted among his Luciferian brethren as their grand link with the nobility of the realm. The dandies of the day knew him by name, as well as sight; and Juliet was a ninny to inquire "What's in a name?"—or rather, Romeo was a blockhead not to reply, "*Everything!*"

"Corney, I want my carriage!" "Corney, call my cab!" "Corney, fetch my fellow!" "Corney, a coach!" distinguished the popular Linkman above his fellows. In vain did the more officious interpose at play or opera; "No—no!—I want Corney Cregan!"— was all the reply vouchsafed to their envious interference.

Corney was now at the top of his profession; Corney had put money in his purse; Corney was a man well to do in the world. It came to be known among the *roués* that Corney had always a five-pound note or two, in his pocket-book, at the Fives-Court, or Epsom, or Ascot, to lend to a customer whose funds might run short; and such little obligations were sure to be handsomely acknowledged on payment of the debt.

Let it not be inferred that our Linkman was guilty of usurious practices. So far from it, that he is recorded to have been as mild and gentlemanly a creditor, as Duval a highwayman. But his amiable forbearance brought its own reward. "Here are a couple of guineas for you, Corney, because you did not plague me!" was by no means an uncommon mode of doing business with the only banker who ever made light of an obligation.

Amid all this flush of prosperity, Cregan considered it his duty to posterity to take a wife. He even asked the opinion and advice of Captain Wrottesley on the subject,—a week after he had become the happy husband of little Katty O'Callaghan.

But if somewhat late in the day for the captain's counsels to be useful, his assistance was not wanting to the poor fellow to whose fortunes his notice had been so providential. Being intimately acquainted with the kind-hearted man, at that period lessee of the King's Theatre, the young patron obtained for Corney the situation of porter to the Opera; and thenceforward, the eyes of Katty and admiring London saluted Mr. Cregan arrayed in a handsome dark blue livery, and a dignity of deportment suitable to so responsible an office.

"Bless your kind heart, Captain Wrottesley, sir!"—said he, addressing his patron at the close of his first season, "only till me how I can sarve ye!—I ben't proud, sir!—Order me as ye plase. For *you*, sir, I shall always be Corney Cragan!"—

Under these happy auspices were a little Katty and a little Corney born to the thriving couple. Corney had his salary and his quarter-day, like other Ministers of State. But unluckily, like other Ministers of State, he ran the hazard of a downfall. Managers, like captains, are casual things. The Opera was more brilliant than ever; the theatre constantly crammed; and the result was, the Gazette and Basinghall Street for the first Lord of its Treasury, and loss of office to one whose letters were now occasionally directed, Cornelius Cregan, Esq.

There was nothing left for it but to give up the cottage at Hampstead, pigstye, strawberry bed and all, and re-enter the modest ranks of private life. Cornelius gazed wistfully upon the miniature Katty and Corney adorning his fireside, and, with a spirit of magnanimity worthy of Coriolanus, became Corney again. It was as though Louis Philippe were to secede from the throne of France, and become once more Duke of Orleans for the benefit of his interesting family!

It was a trying moment—the first night on which Corney took his station once more among his quondam confraternity, his humble link in hand!—Flesh is frail. Linkmen, though enlightened men, are but mortals; and it must be admitted that certain among them, jealous of his recent dignities, wagged their heads, saying, "This our brother, who exalted himself, being abased, is come to take the bread from our mouths, and the mouths of our children!"

It was not till he had made them fully understand that he was a ruined man,—a beggar like themselves,—one who, like Dogberry, had "had losses,"—his whole amount of savings having been invested in the hazardous speculation which engulphed his place and his profits,—that they forgave him his elevation, and forgave him his downfal,—welcoming him cordially again to the world of flambeaux.

Such is the history of Corney Cregan, the tulip of links,—who may be regarded as the Doctor Johnson of the vernacular of slang. Corney is now a veteran. He can no longer call a coach in the brilliant and original style that was wont to excite the plaudits of the stand, when Hughes Ball was a dandy, and Brummell a wit. He is considered, however, the father of the links. His testimony has been more than once invoked in perplexing cases by the sitting magistrates, as the most trustworthy witness in cases of carriage breaking, or footman-slaying, amid the crush of fashionable fêtes. For Corney is known to be a man of honour, the Bayard of the kennel, as well as its admirable Crichton.

Astonishing is the reverence shown him by the rising generation. Whenever a linkboy picks up a diamond cross in the mud, or receives a sovereign in place of a shilling from some reeling swell, it is in the hands of Corney Cregan the treasure is deposited till the question of property can be established.

Corney is king of the elective monarchy of Links. Though not pensioned as an ex-porter, like others as ex-chancellors, he retains out of place almost all the consideration he enjoyed in his dark-blue livery.

There is something imposing in his bassoon-like tones when gratuitously vociferating such names as those of the "Duke of Wellington," or the "Countess of Jersey," when their footmen are missing at some gay entertainment. The intonation of Corney has a character as classically distinct from that of inferior links, as the enunciation of Kemble from that of the romantic schools of modern tragedians. For Corney is the noblest Roman of them all, as well as a link of some value in the chain of modern enlightenment.

The Standard Footman

No one foresaw the future author of Macbeth, in little Will Shakspeare, the wool comber. No one surmised Sir Isaac Newton, in the cunning little Isaac, chary of his tops and marbles. But, in the gaunt lanky footboy of twelve shooting up, like a bean-stalk in the fairy tale, in spite of the wants and miseries that ought to keep him flat and compact, many a starving mother of the lower classes foresees a STANDARD FOOTMAN!

The standard footman is the man of genius of humble life, where the only esprit recognised is *l'esprit du corps*. The standard footman is the Lovelace of the kennel,—the Rochester of the area-gate. If the link-boy afford a striking burlesque of the Page of chivalry, the standard footman is its esquire;—a parody on the beau of old comedy, the Lord Foppington of the stage.

He is, in fact, the only *Marquis* (as a *Marquis* was painted by Molière), extant in Great Britain. The standard footman has "a livery more guarded than his fellows." His wages, which he calls a salary, double theirs. Yet he is as in debt as invariably in love; deep in the books of his laundress,—deep in the affections of the linen-draper's daughter, who would feign disgrace her family, and descend from the dignities of the counter to become his wife. "For bless you!" as her neighbours say, "what can she be a-thinking on?—Richard ben't by no means a marrying man!"

The only falling off, by the way, in the vocation of the standard footman, is this same Richardism. In France, in the days of magnificence, when palaces were constructed like Versailles, tragedies like Bajazet, and comedies like the Tartuffe, great people had ant-hills of lackeys in their households, who clung behind their coaches and six, on gala days, and ran errands in the absence of that modern locomotive conveniency, the post.

But in those grandiose times, aristocratic mouths disdained to pronounce familiarly the vulgar appellations bestowed by god-fathers and godmothers, at the baptismal font.

When a man's name was John, they call'd him,

not " Richard," but "Frontin." Their lackeys were their hereditary vassals. Their lackeys, who were of the earth, earthy—a mere part and parcel of the clay of their estates, were named instead of Tom or Harry, "Champagne," "Lorrain," "Picard," according to their province; or Jasmin, or La Fleur, according to their valet de chambrehood.

There was vast magniloquence in this.—"York, you're wanted!" or, "send Gloucester or Dorset to me," would certainly have a grander sound than "I rang for John." "Call Northumberland!" carries with it a Shakspearian twang; and never more so, than if applied to a stalwart, well-drilled, standard footman.

Premising, however, that for the present these esquires of the aristocratic body are still called Robert or Richard, ("two pretty men,") it may be observed that the man born for the honours of a chariot in Grosvenor Square, is fated to begin a life of servitude with gloomy prospects. The standard footman is sure to have been in his time an overgrown, lanky boy—a diminutive sign-post or clothes horse, with the action of a telegraph, or Irish member. No chance for *him* of the boudoir education of pagehood. At fourteen, he is a great awkward hulk, with uncouth limbs and features, whose only hope of preferment is by enlisting in the household brigade. But his awkwardness and uncouthness are that of a scaffolding promising the standard footman hereafter.

Even such a scaffolding was Tom Scroggs; one of seven sturdy little savages abiding in the cottage of Thomas Scroggs the elder, a locksman on the Paddington canal, domiciled in one of the squalid hovels on Boxmoor, ere Boxmoor became a land of railroads. The mother was a straw-plaiter, according to the custom of the county of Herts; and her children, as soon as their little fingers could move, were taught to fidget between them the coarse rushes of the moor, as a preliminary to the fair and glossy straws which, at some future time, were to be enwoven by them for the Dunstable market.

All was plaiting in the hovel. The children seemed born neat-fingered and adroit. As the spinners of Hindostan possess a peculiar organization of the finger tips, enabling them to draw out the filmy threads that constitute the beauty of India muslin, the Hertfordshire children possess an hereditary instinct for the manual jerk which accomplishes a first-rate straw-plaiter.

Tom, however, the second boy, was an exception. Tom rebelled against this sedentary employment. Tom had a soul above straws. At twelve years old, he was a Patagonian, towering above his brothers and sisters, and threatening some danger to the bare rafters of his low-browed dwelling; the cobwebs pendent whereunto being fanned hither and thither as he traversed the clay-floored chamber, "which served them for kitchen, for parlour, and all."

It is a charming theme for elegiac poets to versify upon the union of poverty and content. Let them only try it for a year or two!—Let them observe face to face the contentment of the poor. Sickness and need are peevish visitations; and Thomas Scroggs and Martha Scroggs were accordingly as cross a pair of parents as any Earl or Countess in Grosvenor Square, harassed by sons who choose to marry to please themselves, and daughters who do not please to marry at all. The mother was a scold, the father a brute; and Mr. and Mrs. Scroggs cuffed their offspring *ad libitum*, whenever they wanted courage to scold and cuff each other; or perhaps for the sake of variety. For their life was not chequered with much pastime. They had no plays or operas to resort to for diversion; and, under such circumstances, a domestic row constitutes an agreeable excitement.

Tom, however, was of a contrary opinion; and, at length determined on deserting the hovel whose bread was at once so hard and scanty, but whose words and blows, though equally hard, were superabundant. He was a bad straw-plaiter. But there was no reason, he thought, that a frame so robust as his might not prove expert at some more manly calling. The Sunday-school at Two-Waters had made a scholar of him; that is, he could write his own name, and spell other people's when written, without much difficulty; and entertained little doubt (at fourteen years of age who does?) of being able to make his way in the world.

Most people have a vein of poetry in their souls, if they only knew where to find it. The silver thread in the iron or brazen nature of Tom Scroggs was a fond affection for a little sister two years younger than himself; a blue-eyed, flaxen-haired, diminutive creature, the most adroit of the hereditary race of straw-plaiters.

To quit little Mary without a word of farewell, was out of the question; and the word farewell, the first he had ever had occasion to utter, brought a flood of tears. Tears purify the stubborn heart, as dew freshens the flower, and even the weed; and, in the moment of tenderness following this expansion of spirit, Tom confided all to his sister!

Now Mary was meek-spirited, and trembled for her brother. Stories of runaway children form the romance of the humble hearth-side; and in the agony of her little bursting heart she rose betimes from the straw-pallet shared by their younger sisters, and went and told her tale to her parents, that they might intercept the escape of Master Thomas.

The father's first impulse was, of course, to inflict such chastisement upon the boy as might render his distasteful home still more distasteful. But, after the severe thrashing which he knew would render escape impossible for a time, Scroggs the elder made proof that second thoughts are best, by proceeding to the neighbouring paper-mill, and obtaining for his uncouth offspring occupation in the factory. Before the day was up, the gaunt lad was established as an extra errand-boy, on the ground, perhaps, of having for his years the longest legs in the parish.

The clumsy delinquent was by degrees promoted to the honour of blacking shoes and cleaning knives, to the relief of the parlour-maid, who waited at table in the establishment. But he was still too great a Yahoo to be admitted to an ostensible share of her labours. The manufacturer's wife, though far from a fine lady, saw the impossibility of producing before company, as her foot-page, a Hottentot, the sleeves of whose fustian jacket, and the legs of whose fustian trousers were always a world too short for his tremendous elongation.

At sixteen, Tom was still an unlicked cub. He was the odd man, that is the odd boy, of the household; worked in the garden, fed rabbits, split wood, went on errands,—no matter what; but still he was so gigantic for his years that these puerile occupations appeared as little suitable to him as the distaff of Omphale to the hands of the great club-man of the antique world.

Don Juan or Byron—for Don Juan is but the comic mask of the noble poet, as Childe Harold his tragic one, assures us that

> 'Tis pleasant to be school'd in a strange tongue
> By female lips and eyes.

In humble life, it is perhaps equally agreeable to be instructed in the folding of table cloths, and filling of salt-cellars, by female hands. The severest butler, the most barbarous groom of the chambers, would not have made so accomplished a scholar of Scroggs junior, as the burnished, bustling, little damsel, whose cherry-coloured cheeks vied with her cherry-coloured ribands, officiating as commander-in-chief in the pantry of the paper-mill. Maria's chidings were so much like praise!—Maria's chidings of the errand-boy's awkwardness being, of course, just as coquettish in their way, as the *agaceries* of a young lady in her third London season, touching the little faults of a raw ensign in the Guards,—that is, a raw ensign having a handsome face or handsome fortune!—The ensign in the Guards so piquantly chided, becomes a dandy; the cub so charmingly cuffed, an accomplished footman.

Thus pleasantly passed the tenour of Tom Scroggs's days; including the Sundays which, by permission of his Pharaoh of the mill, were usually spent in wandering about the green lanes by Gadesbridge or Gaddesden, with his sisters; the straw-bonnet of his darling Mary being twisted round with a garland of woodbine or wild clematis, or hazel-nuts, pulled for her by his high-reaching hand. Succeeding years might have worn away with little vicissitude, save those of summer and winter, spring and autumn, which changed the garlands from green wheat-ears to yellow, or the bouquets from bundles of violets to bundles of cornflowers,—when, lo! some malicious influence willed that the gaunt errand-boy of the paper-mill should be despatched with a packet of stationery to the steward's room, or office, of Ashbridge Castle—the Windsor of the neighbourhood of Boxmoor.

From his boyhood, on occasions of battues in the woods, Tom Scroggs had made his way into those aristocratic precincts had penetrated into the green grassy dells, and gazed with admiring eyes upon the herded deer gathered under their drooping beech-trees, the pride of the neighbourhood.

But he had never approached the house, then but recently completed. To him it was as a majestic and forbidden palace— magical in its structure as that of Aladdin;—a thing to dream of in awe and rapture, as the eternal palace of the Unspeakable.

But upon this occasion, he was privileged to "pass the guards, the gates, the wall;"—to penetrate the courts, both outer and inner, and finally make way into the domestic offices of the potentate so great in his eyes, to whom his burthen was addressed, as "The Right Honourable Earl of Bridgewater."

On his way, the eye of the young errand-man caught a glimpse of a terrestrial Paradise beyond all his former imaginings!

On the smooth shaven lawn before the long Gothic front of the hall, the white freestone of which was carved and pierced as though minarets of Brussels lace were uplifted in the air,—on the smooth-shaven green as though one entire and perfect emerald lay extended in the sunshine, or rather, not an emerald, but a soft expanse of verdant velvet, worthy the foot of a queen, and the tripsome steps of her lovely ladies of honour,—on the smooth-shaven lawn, was a wicket set up; and lo! a group of well-made, well-dressed individuals, in nankeen tights and silk stockings, and shirts of snowy whiteness, were indulging in the midsummer pastime of cricket!

For a moment, Tom Scroggs entertained little doubt that these gentlemen whose laughter was ringing in the air, while their balls were bounding along the green, could be none other than the goodly sons of the Earl (albeit, sons he had none), or Members of Parliament, or great lords, or perhaps captains of the armies of the King.

But, on comparing the nankeen tights and woven silk enveloping their lower man, with the nankeen tights and woven silk adorning the extremities of certain bystanders, over whose shirts were still buttoned the livery coats of the house of Egerton, Tom Scroggs perceived that the cricketers were none other than the lackeys of Lord Bridgewater, disporting themselves according to their custom of an afternoon, and the benign permission of the venerable Earl and Countess.

Wandering towards an iron garden-fence hard by, his eye caught sight of the coats which had been flung aside by the heroes *in cuerpo*, so much greater men *without* their laced jackets than with them. Spruce, lustrous, joyous, well powdered as they were, they were simply footmen:—not angels, but footmen!

From that moment, Tom dreamed only of a livery. From that moment, footmen became in his imagination,

> gay creatures of the elements,
> That in the colours of the rainbow live;

happy individuals in nankeen tights and shirts of fine Irish; whose chief occupation in the household of an Earl is to play cricket on a green lawn alternated with shade and sunshine by quivering beech-trees.

Tom had never been in London; never heard

> the rattle of street-pacing steeds,—

nor the rat-tat-too of a footman's thundering rap. Vigils, cares, watchings, waitings, were mysteries to *him*!

But be it freely admitted that Tom Scroggs, like Cæsar, was ambitious. He began to loathe the sight, sound, and smell of the mill. He despised the simple suits and simpler manners of the workmen. Assuming the folly of Malvolio, he could think of nothing but lords and ladies. To tread evermore upon smooth lawns or smoother carpets,—to play everlastingly cricket and the fool,—oh happy fate!—oh! thrice, thrice happy footmen!

Tom, though a rebellious, had not been a bad son. From the period of his having wages at command, they were transferred to the house on Boxmoor; and sister Mary had now a handsome shawl for Sundays to enhance the simplicities of her straw-bonnet.

But thenceforward he was generous no longer. He had become an egotist,—the first step towards becoming a great man. As a preliminary to silk hose, he made a purchase of cotton ones to replace on Sundays his coarse, speckled worsted stockings; and became, by one, by two, and by three, a man of many shirts.

By degrees his wardrobe grew and grew; and, though it contained nothing which the gentleman in nankeen summer-tights would not have consigned to the flames or the old clothes' shop, it was as dawning of dandyism to the Hertfordshire clown.

An ambitions mind is not disposed to let "I dare not, wait upon I would." Tom was well aware that a livery would not fall, like the prophet's mantle, on his shoulders, while he stood gazing afar off upon the splendour of Ashbridge Castle; and, after much heart-aching and head-aching, yearning and spurning, aspiring and desiring, Tom Scroggs gave warning at the mill, and came straight to town, where his handsome person and a four years' character procured him a situation as second footman in the family of a wealthy cit, not too choice in the graces of his lackeys. A firm, active, good young man, to go behind Mrs. Graham's blue coach with red wheels, in a green livery, and help to wait at table at his villa at Edmonton, was all he wanted; and Scroggs was the man for his money. "Thomas was the civilest fellow in the world. Thomas was a trump!"

All this was miles and miles distant from the nankeen tights and greensward of Ashbridge;—and the soul of genius was burning within the body of Thomas, and consuming it away. Nothing like a secret grief for refining the mind and manners! In the pantry of the Grahams, the pensive youth sat and dreamed of the West End. No boy-member, conscious of the inspirations of a Fox or a Burke, ever sighed more wofully after distinction. The blue coach and, its modest cipher were loathsome in his sight. He wanted coronets and supporters. He wanted a simple livery, in place of the spinach-coloured coat, and the lace wherewith he was bedizened. He wanted levees, he wanted drawing-rooms—at which to display his noble proportions.

There does not exist an object of modern art, or an adjunct of modern civilization, more exclusively and peculiarly artificial, than the London chariot of some fashionable English duchess. A *bijou*, in all but dimensions, the ease of its movements, smooth as the address of a ministerial candidate,— the lustre of its component parts, polished as the manners of a Lord Chamberlain,—the precision, elegance, symmetry, and proportion of its distribution,—the blood horses,—the harness so light, and yet so heavy,—the coachman in his snow-white wig and cocked hat, so ponderous, yet so light of hand,—the elastic cushions, with their pale delicate silk lace, the polished ivory handles,—the fleecy rug,—the resplendent panels,—the varnish, black as jet,—are glorious attributes of the life that begins at two o'clock in the day, and end at four o'clock in the morning!

The best part of the town chariot, however, consists decidedly in its brace of standard footmen. A pair of anything—saving a matrimonial pair—is sure to have an harmonious appearance. A pair of pictures, a pair of statues, a pair of vases, a pair of consoles, a pair of shells, sells for fourfold the money of the same objects, single. There is something in the words "a good match" agreeable to other ears besides the mothers of many daughters. Most things in nature are of the dual number. Substance bears its shadow,—its echo;—and happiness is by no means the only abstract sentiment that is "born a twin."

But of all the happy pairs in creation, few are more agreeable to the eye than a pair of standard footmen. Sportsmen, accustomed to talk of partridges and Mantons, usually say brace;—but pair comes more glibly. A pair of standard footmen seems to be the real pair of inexpressibles.

For many years, it was the custom of every servants hall to have its hiring-stand, whereby the altitude of the footman presenting himself for an engagement, was decided. *Mais nous avons changé tout cela.* Now-a-days, a box is set up, compact as a coffin, in which the absolute dimensions of the appendage to the town chariot, are minutely verified;—so many inches across the shoulders,—in girth so much, and so forth. The match must be as exact as that of a pair of Shetland ponies destined to run in a royal carriage. Even complexion and whiskers come into the account; and last season, it transpired that one of the most elegant and fashionable countesses of the day had sent for her apothecary, and placed one of her standard footmen under as severe a course of medicine and regimen as though he had been about to run for the Derby, because he was outgrowing his measure, and was too accomplished a fellow to be dismissed from her service for obesity. It was an easier affair to starve him down, than replace him.

Bitter was the anguish of spirit with which the Thomas of the Barbican contemplated these aristocrats of the shoulder-knot, as they flitted past him, mounted on their monkey-boards, behind the brilliant equipages of the season.

Everybody knows who looks at a balloon, that it is destined for the skies; and everybody knew who looked at Thomas that he was assured of the future honours of the standard. But the air-balloon takes a terrible long time in the filling; exposed to endless bumpings and thumpings in the contest between its skyward and earthward tendency. Equally percussive were the changes of Tom Scroggs's fortunes, while vibrating between the East end and the West.

Suffice it for posterity that, in the twenty-third year of his age,—this boy premier, this Pitt of the shoulder established as the second of the two helots in blue and gold of the fashionable young Countess of Frothington, in Carlton Gardens;—the most accomplished of his vocation,—the Trip of living life.

Never was there such a Thomas seen as *our* Thomas;—

——a creature
Framed in the very poetry of nature;

a picture of a standard footman; a man who might have preceded the
sedan of Lady Teazle or the beautiful Lady Coventry; or delivered
in the ticket of the fairest of duchesses, at Hastings's trial.

Where had he attained all these accomplishments? There is a
college in Normandy for the education of learned poodles, where
they take degrees as bachelors of the arts of telling fortunes on
cards, or become Doctors Bowwowring. But *is* there within the
bills of mortality a school for the perfecting of footmen? A poet is
born a poet;—a standard footman can scarcely be born a standard
footman;—or, at all events, little Tom Scroggs was not born the
unequalled Thomas of Carlton Gardens.

Imagine the marble of the Apollo Belvedere mollified by a
tepid bath, and dressed by Meyer or Curlewis in a suit fitting as
close as the glove of an *élégante* of the Chaussée d'Antin, or the
calyx of a rose bud!—Imagine a head powdered and perfumed like
that of Fleury in the part of some charming Marquis!—Imagine a
cocked-hat with its silver-lace and tassels so nicely balanced over
the well-powdered head, that if " zephyr blowing underneath the
violet, not wagging its sweet head," had chosen to have a blow at
the head of Thomas, it must have been blown over.

No need to dwell upon the whiskers, arranged in tiers of curls,
five tiers in the right whisker and four in the left, according to
the fashion of the most memorable coxcomb of the day. No need
to enlarge upon a complexion which perhaps owed something
to the Kalydor and Gowland, said by Lord Frothington's *valet
de chambre* to disappear in a most mysterious manner from
his lordship's toilet-table, with his orange-flower pomatum and
bouquet de verveine. No need to describe the fit of a varnished
shoe, "small by degrees, and beautifully less," at the extremity of a
manly leg, vying with that of Pam on a court card.

For the distinctions of Thomas were not solely physical.
Thomas was a Rochester in refinement of mind as well as body.

For four preceding years, Thomas had made the Morning Post his daily study, and the Peerage and Baronetage his Sunday reading. Thomas knew what was what, and who was whom;—everybody by name who *had* a name, and anybody by sight worthy to meet the eyes of a standard footman.

Whatever carriage might roll to the door in Carlton Gardens,— for its footman to deliver the name of the visitors was wholly superfluous. The Heralds' college could not have produced a more cunning interpreter of arms and liveries than Thomas. He was a living Court Guide, an ambulatory Directory. No sooner had two syllables of the name of the person she intended to visit escaped the lips of the young Countess of Frothington, than Thomas was perched behind the chariot beside Henry, like twin Mercuries "new lighted on a heaven-kissing hill," while a distinct enunciation, "clear as a trumpet with a silver sound," conveyed instructions to the coach man. Off, like an arrow from a bow, went the carriage; obeying, like the magic horse of a fairy tale, the scarcely expressed wishes of its lovely mistress—the spell being breathed by the accomplished lips of Thomas.

It has been hinted, that Lady Frothington's two Trips were so Machiavelic in their policy, so perfect in their tact, as to know precisely at what part of the file of carriages at the Opera, Almack's, or other balls, to place her ladyship's chariot, so as to be within reach at the precise moment they were likely to be called for. They were supposed to be able to infer, to a second, at what o'clock the Countess was likely to be bored, according to the carriages and cabriolets in waiting; or the likelihood of a division in the House of Commons; or the claims of a party at the palace.

On observing, for instance, the pretty Viscountess alight from her carriage, attired in her châtelaine of diamonds, when his own lady happened to wear only flowers or turquoises. Certain that the Countess would shrink from being overblazed, Thomas, hastened to bring up Lady Frothington's equipage within ready reach, and kept as close to the door as was compatible with the unsavoury odours of the linkmen and other fractions of the populace who congregate at the heels of the police, wherever lords and ladies assemble together for the purpose of sitting through a ball, or talking through a concert.

The moment a certain cabriolet was seen to drive up, on the other hand, and deposit one of the most popular of aristocratic dandies, Thomas would intimate to the coachman that he might retire to the opposite side of the square, or end of the street, and enjoy his two hours' snooze, unmolested by the coughing of horses, the smashing of panels, or the snoring of his brother whips.—Exact as an astronomer's calculations of a planet's rising and setting, were those of the standard footman touching the duration of the flirtations of her ladyship.

In former times, in the old-fashioned halls of our family mansions, the domestics of visitors were allowed to sit down and wait for their masters and mistresses,—for the season being then winter, the footmen would have run some chance of being frozen to death at the doors; and highly offensive were the results of a practice which compelled young and gentle ladies to confront the ordeal of their insolent stare and vulgar comments, on their way to the uncloaking room.

Now, it is considered that the insolent stare and vulgar comments of the dandies above, are sufficient; and few and quizzical are the houses where the livery of London is admitted beyond the threshold. A modern vestibule, delicately carpeted and filled with exotics, is a far more appropriate portico to the temple of pleasure, than a hall full of dusty or damp livery-servants.

Now that the regulations of the police are as accurate as the scapements of clockwork,—now that the London season commences with the strawberries, and ends with pheasant-shooting,—the appropriate place for footmen is the pavement, or the coach-box, over the opposite corners of whose hammercloth the twin Mercuries swing their legs and canes on either side of Coachy, like genii perched upon the marble angles of a monument in Westminster Abbey.

> There they talk,—
> Ye gods, how they do talk,—

of the state of the nation,—the state of lords and ladies,—the state of ladies who love their lords, and lords who love their ladies.

They know everything,—they say everything. With *them* no delicate hints,—no slight insinuations,—no shirking a question, or diplomatising an answer. They are in everybody's secrets. My lady can only surmise the mysteries of my lord, or my lord those of my lady. Their footmen are at the bottom of both. Their footmen have compared notes with the footmen who bring their notes however cautiously the secret may have been worded in the morning, it is sure to be blurted out without reserve, at night, between the accomplished gentleman in blue and gold, and the accomplished gentleman in silver and white.

At the gate of Kensington Gardens, or the Zoological Gardens, or *déjeûners*, or exhibitions, day after day, a meeting assembles like that of the Scientific Association, calculated to bring all things to light. The gossip of one fashionable dinner-table, alone, within ear-shot of three or four first-rate Thomases, is sufficient to disperse throughout the town rumours enough to set a hundred families of consideration into a ferment.

Perhaps the most fastidious gentleman now extant is the standard footman. The style in which he surveys a snobby equipage,—or answers the "Lady Frothington at home?" of some stunted Richard in a quizzical livery, the armorial bearings correspondent with which have neither place nor station in Debrett or Lodge, might form a study for the less impertinent scorners of Crockford's.

The eye of half vacant wonder with which he contrives to express his amazement that such *very* obscure individuals should exist in the world, and such very detestable equipages be allowed to go about; and the extraordinary flexibility of feature whereby he conveys his utter alienation and estrangement of nature from the animal who affects confraternization with him, because also arrayed in a parti-coloured coat, —is beyond all praise. Brummell could not have done it better, when wreaking his dandified contempts upon his "fat friend" George the Fourth.

In this superlative exquisitism of the shoulder-knot, the Thomas of Carlton Gardens excelled.

"Going to Willis's with your vouchers? Then pray change ours for me," said a certain James, the Trip of Lady R., a banker's lady of Cavendish Square, on meeting Lady Frothington's Trip in the neighbourhood of King Street, one Wednesday morning.

"*Weeleeses?*" ejaculated Thomas, with a countenance calculated to turn sour, all the cream in Grange's shop,—"of what are you talking? My dear fellow,—you don't suppose *we* go to Almack's?—Her ladyship refused the patroness-ship last season. Almack's is vastly well to bring out squire's daughters, or push the acquaintance of banker's wives; but WE have given it up these two years."

Thomas is an epicure as well as a dandy. Thomas never tastes ice of anything but fresh strawberries, after March. When accompanying other Thomases to the doors of "dealers in British compounds," (while waiting for her ladyship at those privileged parties, when the carriage is despatched to the other end of the street or side of the square) Thomas is scrupulously careful to quaff, in a tumbler, the brown stout which less fastidious flunkeys are satisfied to swallow from the pewter.

Nor would Thomas derange the set of his well-starched cravat, by turning round to look at the prettiest nursery-maid tripping down the steps of Canton Gardens into the park; the plait of his shirt-frill being quite as much an object to him, as to any of the irresistibles who have given to the fashionable clubs the aspect of milliner's shops.

Thomas is not aware of the existence of the multitudinous untitled, saving as the populace." He talks about "the people" as being never contented; and wonders what all this rubbish can mean about the repeal of the Corn Laws. As he steps jauntily across the kennel, with his hat on one side, and his thumb jerked negligently into his waistcoat, on his way to deliver a note to the handsome young Marquis, Thomas is fifty times as fine a gentleman as any one of the heroes of the nankeen tights.

But who on earth would ever detect the ragged urchin of Boxmoor in this essenced fop,—this sunny epicurean!—who would ever surmise the lanky errand-boy of the mill at Two-Waters, in Lady Frothington's STANDARD FOOTMAN?

The Lady's-Maid

THE NAME BESTOWED BY MODERN parlance upon the waiting or tirewoman, denotes youth and jauntiness. The very word "maid" seems to anticipate the qualifying adjection of "fair" or "pretty," as naturally as in the polite circles of Austria, the word "*frau*" receives the prefix of "*gnädige*." And though it must be admitted that toothless and grey-haired wives and widows often pass under the general designation of ladies' maids, it is still held an essential distinction of lady's-maidism, to possess a pleasing exterior.

The lady's-maid is the flower of the domestic establishment,—the Proserpine of the lower regions,—the *élégante*, whose graces of mind and manners bewilder the minds of the footmen, to whom, with supercilious scorn she delivers the orders of her principals;—a stumbling-block in the eyes of venerable butlers, as Maria in those of Malvolio, and a target for the merry jests of the servants' hall.

The lady's-maid is my lady's shadow; a parody upon the *chef-d'oeuvre* of elegance, to whose cast-off clothes, airs, and graces, she has the honour to succeed. Though worn to the bone by the labours of office,—though deprived of her rest by my lady's dissipation, and of her meals by my lady's selfishness,—though harassed by flaws of temper and caprices of taste, there is a species of one and indivisibility between the mistress and maid, characteristic of the umbrageous nature pointed out. An instinctive *esprit de corps* unites the daughter of Eve who washes the laces, and is to inherit them, with the daughter of Eve who wears them in her pinners.

Against my master, or my lord, on the other hand, the lady's-maid cherishes an intuitive antipathy. Even my master's own man,—nay, even the family butler, and coachman does she detest, as dependencies of "master." "Master," is a tyrant,—master is a nuisance,—master is never satisfied,—master is always complaining of the manner in which his linen is starched, or left unstarched; and master's shirt-buttons have twice as great an aptitude to come off as any other gentleman's.

And then, master keeps such hours! Master goes to bed, and rises earlier than can be accounted for on any other principle than that of matrimonial contrariety. Master comes into my lady's dressing-room in dirty boots; or sets down his flat candlestick on a new cap. Master is full of fancies,—such as having his newspapers ironed; and worrets people out of their lives about keeping dinner or horses waiting. According to the lady's-maid there is no end to the peccadillos of "master."

Not but that my lady has her faults too. My lady is sadly thoughtless and heedless and seems to think people have twenty pair of hands, and no need of rest or recreation. But she is such a good creature, after all! And, if it were not for having such a brute of a husband, she would be such a sweet-tempered lady.—Ah! poor thing! if people only knew what they were about when they married!

The lady's-maid swears she would not change her situation for anything that anybody could offer her; that is, her situation in life. As regards her vocation, it must be admitted that she enjoys peculiar advantages. Other slaveys occupy the post of Tantalus. The butler is no wise privileged to be the better for the wine he is decanting, or the plate he is cleaning; or the gardener for the pines or peaches he is forcing. But if the task of the lady's-maid be an eternal smoothing of coats, and darning of pinholes, *she* at least has a vested interest in the fruit of her labours. The lawn kerchief, or brocaded mantle, will one day be her own; and the young heir who watches the growth of his father's plantations, is not more personally interested in their well-doing, than the lady's-maid in the safe packing of her lady's imperials and chaise-seat.

The lady's-maid is usually an hysterical, nervous personage. Her constitution is broken by irregular rest and irregular diet. Addicted to novels and green tea, she is not aware that her tender hypochondriacism is the result of swallowing her dinner whole, to be in time for dressing my lady for her daily drive; and of restless nights, spent in watching at the dressing-room window for the return of my lady's carriage from the ball. On the contrary, she admits that she is a poor, weak-spirited creature; but swears, like Cassio, that she "had it from her mother."

It is a strange thing that, howbeit, we all admit the difficulty of being a hero to one's *valet de chambre*, or an angel to one's lady's maid,—every lady insists upon the maid being an angel to her lady. The mistress has a right to be *en déshabille* at certain hours of the day. The maid never. The maid must be always presentable,—always smiling. Curl-papers are warning, and a slipshod foot dismissal without a character. Whether in drawing my lady's curtain at dead of night, or undrawing it at daybreak, she must be *tirée à quatre épingles*, and neither look fatigued, nor restless, nor sick, nor sorry. A weary eye, or a pale face, would condemn her to hear that "her health was not equal to her situation." For with the exception of an inquisitor of Spain, there are few things more cruel than a fine lady.

Having laid it down as an axiom that a lady's-maid is simply her lady's shadow, it is almost unnecessary to add, that there are as many varieties of ladies' maids as of roses and geraniums serious ladies' maids, fashionable ladies' maids, ladies' maids on their preferment, flirting ladies' maids,—and so forth.

The serious lady's maid is pretty sure to be privately married to the butler, or to have a weakness for the under-footman. The fashionable lady's maid is above such vulgarisms; talks of "the circle she moves in," and goes to the Opera. The lady's maid on her preferment, converts my lady's cast off satins and *guipures* into cash, and talks of her property in the funds. While the flirting lady's-maid converts them to her own use; has a correspondence in verse with one of the young gentlemen at Howell and James's,

which does not prevent her lending an ear to a thousand tender
nothings when the country-house is full of dandies, masters, and
men, for the hunting and shooting season.

Most of these flutterlings of the basement story dote upon
London and the season. Despite their vigils and wearyings, they
love the stir and movement of that sunny period when my lady's
diamonds emerge from their morocco cases, and every day brings
home some new dress, bonnet, or cap, creaking up the back stairs
in the milliner's basket. They love the noise, glitter, and outlay of
such a time. They delight in gauds of silver and gold, and all the
intertanglements of pink, blue, and lilac, devised by haberdashers
for the perdition of the female kind. A new ribbon distracts them
as a vacant riband the sovereign.

The Drawing Room is the grand event of the lady's-maid.
"My lady looks so very sweet in her feathers, lappets, and family
diamonds; and the *real* lady is never more distinguishable from
the upstart than in her train and point!" An unusual flush mantles
on her cheek as she indulges in the plebeian vice of gazing out
of the window upon the departing chariot, with its well-wigged
coachman, and pair of standard footmen, alike as the two
Antipholi, or as Dromio and his *fac-simile*, to the very buckles in
their shoes, and bouquets in their button holes. She is conscious
of having sent forth my lady to go, see, and conquer; proud that
the labour of her hands should figure in presence of the court.

Though selectly select in her visiting-list, her acquaintance
in town is considerable; and the best mansions in May-Fair
contribute their quota of ladies'-maids to her whist-table on
Opera nights, or royal ball nights, when she is sure of getting rid
of my lady at an early hour.

The Dowager Duchess's maid, on the other hand, steps in on
Sunday nights, her Grace who is serious and averse to Sabbath
breaking, giving freedom to her men and maid servants on the
Lord's day. But for her own part, she is not averse to the Park or
Kensington Gardens on Sundays, when she can secure a proper
escort; or a trip to Epsom with a subscription carriage, half-and-half
with the Marchioness's people, and the Marquis's champagne and
sandwiches gratis. She owns she loves a little innocent recreation.

Hitherto, the lady's-maid has been described in the single number, and, consequently, in her most amiable form. But, when two or more ladies'-maids are gathered together in one establishment, Heaven have a care of it! Queen Bess, that shrewdest of legislatresses, observed of her royal rival of Scotland, that "the sky would not bear two suns; nor England two queens." Still less, one roof two ladies'-maids!

From the moment my young lady or my young ladies grow up, and require a maid of their own, there is an end of the peace of the establishment. The precedence of the case, indeed, takes care of itself. As a peer walks before a peer's elder son, mamma's maid walks before the maid of her daughters. But the petty jealousies, heresies, and schisms hourly arising in the housekeeper's room, are beyond even the adjustment of the Herald's Office. The sensitive creatures fight for everything; and when there is nothing to be fought for, like an Irishman in a row, fight for nothing. They are at dagger's drawn for the butler's affections, for the merry-thoughts of the chickens, for the middle piece of the toast, for the snuffers, the poker, the newspaper, the date of her Majesty's approaching accouchement, the duration of the next ministry, and the odd trick.—*Bella,—horrida bella!*—Incessant wars and rumours of war,—"war to the curling irons!"

At a fashionable country mansion a visitor once picked up a letter near the offices, containing the reply of the servants of a neighbouring nobleman to an invitation to a steward's-room ball. "Mrs. Simpkins would have the honour of waiting upon Mrs. Spriggins, *but the young ladies'-maid was not yet out.*"

This is the heart of the mystery! The senior lady's-maid is apt to assume airs of chaperonship, to play the dowager,—to rebuke over-tricksomeness of costume,—to call flirting young *valets de chambre* to account, and inquire into their "intentions." The junior consequently rebels, asserts her independence, and will not be put upon. To incrimination follows recrimination. "A few words" ensue; "and if" in words "the more the merrier," the fewer, the bitterer. A strife of ladies' maids is as the wrangling of parrots. With ladies'-maid as with church preferments, therefore, let all right-thinking people eschew pluralities.

But if such the discourse where two or more ladies'-maids are concerned, what shall we say of the envy, hatred, malice, and all uncharitableness, engendered in a house where the dowager's lady's-maid is a sober, middle-aged English waiting gentlewoman, wearing spectacles in the housekeeper's room, and a silk front everywhere; and the junior a little French soubrette, her hair *coiffé en bandeaux*, while the muslin that *ought* to have been converted into a cap, figures in the shape of an embroidered apron.

The senior calls the junior a play-actress; the junior calls the senior a duenna. The young ladies side with Mademoiselle Eugénie, who braids their locks and crisps their ringlets so charmingly, who assures one that she is *gantée à ravir*, and another that she is *chaussée comme un ange*; while the mamma naturally takes part with the Sobersides who has so much sympathy with her rheumatism, and who caps texts with her while arranging the folds of her turban. An intervention and non-intervention war is waged between the parties and Lord Palmerston and Monsieur Thiers are nothing to Mrs. Smallridge and Mademoiselle Eugénie in the punctiliousness of their opposition.

The merry little *femme de chambre*—(for a French lady's maid, though single, assumes in Great Britain womanly designation withheld from her, though double,—the merry little *femme de chambre* runs about the house, only the more enlivened by the feud. Her very work is play to her. She enjoys the idea of the young ladies' balls, even at second-hand. A perpetual course of hair-dressing, frilling, flouncing, and tying of bows, is her *beau idéal* of the duties of life.

Provided "*ces chères demoiselles*" distinguish themselves in society by the elegance of their dress, she is satisfied. She complains of nothing but the want of sunshine and play-going;—of "*ce vilain climat*," and "*cet éternel go-to-shursh*."

Reports of Mademoiselle Eugénie's having proposed a game of *écarté* to the butler on a rainy Sunday afternoon in the country, at length, however, reach the heads of the family, and produce her dismissal; Mrs. Smallridge (who has been reading Tom Jones meanwhile, with locked doors, in her own room) having signified that "matters can't go on in *that* way," and that one or other of them must leave the house. On such grounds, the dowager lady's maid is privileged to be authoritative. Her threat suffices. Even in the best regulated families she has been trusted too much behind the curtain, to be safely trusted before it. Off, therefore, goes poor Mademoiselle; and Mrs. Smallridge thenceforward assumes airs of despotism in the housekeeper's room, such as would not sit amiss upon the Shah of Persia.

We have asserted that it is desirable for the lady's maid to be of a fair presence. But this rule is observable within limitation. A lady's maid may be a vast deal too pretty for her places. We remember one who had indeed a right to the prefix of "fair," and who was fairly ruined by the distinction. She was one of the many who, from being taken out of her own situation in life, become fit for no situation at all,—or, at all, events, become most disagreeably situated.

A cottager's child with a pretty face, and the pretty name of Alice, certain sentimental young ladies who resided in a cottage of gentility in the village, smitten with her pink cheeks and flaxen curls, selected the poor child as a picturesque object whereupon to exercise their benevolent propensities. Half the fair philanthropists labouring in the by-ways of human nature are singularly biased in the selection of their *protégés*, by comeliness and favour; though the ugly ones be far more in need of aid along the thorny place of this brambly world.

But little Alice looked so pretty over her spelling-book or sampler, in the parlour furnished with muslin curtains and faded gilt card-racks, that half the time of the morning visitors was taken up in calling her "sweet dear," and asking whether she were not very grateful to the "kind young ladies" who took so much heed of her; till the child grew vain, unsuspicious that she was only there to minister to the vanity of others. She minded her book a little, but the visitors more; and at twelve years old, knew just enough to be in the way of the young ladies, and out of the way of advancement in life.

Had she been pug-nosed or freckled, and brought up like other ugly girls at the village-school, Alice would have learned scrubbing and plain work, and her services been early available in her family or elsewhere. But on returning at twelve years old, spoiled, to the cottage, she was good for no manner of thing but to be scolded.

She was twitted with the whiteness of her hands and blackness of her disposition, till her pretty blue eyes became of a permanent red with crying; and had not the superior of a sort of Do-the-girls' Hall establishment advertised for a genteel apprentice, and one of the kind young ladies assisted her pupil into the office, by way of getting a troublesome hanger-on still further out of the way, the poor girl would probably have dissolved, like Arethusa, into a fountain of tears.

At the end of her seven years' apprenticeship, pretty Alice was prettier than ever, and almost as helpless. She had acquired a smattering of French, a smattering of fine work, a smattering of personal graces, enough to make a lady's maid, yet not enough to make a governess. Being a very good girl withal,—gentle-hearted, affectionate, modest, simple,—she was sadly afraid of becoming a burthen to her parents, and eager to push her way in the world; and the "kind young ladies," who had now progressed into middle-aged ladies, remembering the former advantage of an advertisement, tried again.

On examining the County Chronicle, "a genteel young person" was again found wanting in the county town, as attendant upon the daughters of the rich banker; whose villa and conservatory, kept at the cost of the place, were its pride and glory.

But after the transportation of Alice, with much difficulty, to be examined as to her qualifications and recommendations by Mrs. Crabstock in person, the pretty maid was dismissed, unexamined. Her fault lay upon the surface. No need for cross-questioning. She was told that she was too young. The letter of explanation she brought back to the kind middle-aged ladies was more candid. Mrs. Crabstock simply observed, "I have several sons."

The kind middle-aged ladies accordingly looked out for a place in a family as exclusively female as their own; and were fortunate in persuading Lady Crossgrain, a wealthy widow, with an only daughter, to receive as second maid a young person of undeniable character, so well brought up as to be almost a companion for Miss Crossgrain. That "almost" was again fatal!—It was a severe winter. Society was scarce at Crossgrain Hall. Pretty Alice was accepted as almost a companion. She was really an acquisition. The simple girl was so genuinely delighted by her young lady's fine playing and fine singing; and stood with such untiring ears to listen!

Unluckily, she looked prettier than ever in that listening attitude. Since the days of Ellen Douglas, no one ever listened half so charmingly; and when at length there arrived from the Continent the tall cousin, Sir Jacob Crossgrain, who, it was intended by her ladyship, should unite the title and estates of the family by an union with the heiress, it became evident that there was not the slightest chance of the consummation so devoutly to be wished, so long as Miss Crossgrain's coarse black locks were seen in contrast with the silken curls of Alice, or the high shoulders of the young lady with the graceful form of the young lady's maid.

Poor Alice was consequently turned adrift again. But, as in conscience bound, the Crossgrains disposed of her discreetly with another widow lady, where there was no daughter to be eclipsed by her charms.

Without offspring to engross her attention, Mrs. Murray had scarcely an object on which to bestow her affections, saving her own face in the glass; and at three-and-forty it is no such pleasant thing for a crowsfooted coquette to find a fair young seraphic visage perpetually reflected over her shoulder, like a moral tacked to the last page of a romance. Nothing more easy than to discover a seam awry in Alice's sewing, and turn her again upon the wide world!

So was it everywhere. Either there were sons, brothers, or nephews, whose hearts and the respectability of the community might be end angered,—or "missus" was of a jealous temper,—or my lady ambitious of remaining the only beauty in the house. Love followed as naturally in the wake of poor Alice as Cupid in that of Venus; and she would have done well to get inoculated with confluent small pox, or tattooed with permanent ink.

It would be painful to pursue the career of so sweet a creature through all its griefs and grievances. Alice is now, at thirty, and sorely against her will, a chorus singer at a minor theatre. Miserable as is her pittance, and degraded her position, it was impossible for so meek a nature to bear up against the insults and hardships heaped upon her as an over-pretty LADY'S-MAID.

The Family Butler

IMPOSSIBLE TO APPROACH WITH TOO grave a step the consideration of a functionary so important as the Family Butler!—Linkmen, and even footmen, are of the populace baptized more or less indelibly with the waters of the kennel. But the butler is a man so many degrees upraised above his origin, as to have cast aside his nature, and in every sense of the word to have forgotten himself. A renegade to gutter-baptism, he has gradually achieved greatness passing all human understanding even his own.

His essential distinction is to be "highly respectable." The family butler is one of the outward and visible graces of every family qualified to *call* itself a family. A footman is only a slovenly half-and-half appendage of gentility. People who live in "houses" keep a footman; people who "reside" in "mansions" superadd a butler, with second, third, fourth, or fifth footmen, as the, case may be. But the butler is indispensable; i.e. indispensable to "family" and "a mansion."

Saving his presence therein, who would there be to drink the last three glasses out of every bottle of port,—the last two out of every bottle of sherry,—and the first of every bottle of Nantes or liqueur? Who would there be to detect an oversight in the brewer's bill of seven-pence-halfpenny to his master's disadvantage, and exact at the same time a mulct of five-and-twenty per cent. in his own favour? Who would there be to complain of the badness of the broadcloth in the liveries sent home from the tailor's;

and interpolate in the bill an item of an odd waistcoat or two, furnished to himself?

The butler may be said to represent the Upper House in an Englishly constituted establishment. The servants' hall stands for the Commons;—the steward's or housekeeper's room for the Lords; or mistress, for the throne; no bill passing to the sign-manual of the latter, without having progressed through the ordeal of the former two.

Of late years, it has been the custom of the Upper House of Parliament to wag its head in the face of royalty, and have a will of its own,—a will equally at variance with those above and those below. It is ever so with the butler; who is pretty sure to be at once his master's master, and his master's servants' master. He is too powerful over the supplies not to make his authority respected. If factiously opposed by the domestics, or fractiously by their proprietor, he contrives to throw the whole weight and labour of the state upon, the shoulders of the latter; and the whole weight and labour of everything else into the hands of the former. When Louis the Fourteenth, in pursuance of his state maxim, "*l'état c'est moi*," took it into his head to become his own minister, Louvois was careful to fling into the portfolio such an agglomeration of state papers, and complication of public business, that, at the close of a few days, his Majesty was right glad to cry for mercy, and beg the cabinet council to do his work for him, as in duty bound.

So is it with the adroit butler, on finding his lord or master impertinently bent upon "looking into things." The cellar-book,—the plate-list—and every other list—(oh! List!)—committed to his administration, made to assume a degree of mysterious complexity, defying the decipherment of Babbage.

Pipes of port, hogsheads of claret, cases of champagne, gallons of spirituous liquors, are unaccountably added up, subtracted, and divided, by the rule of three and the rule of contrary, into Babylonic confusion, such as worse confounds the confusion of the proprietor of all this intolerable quantity of sack. In the end, he throws it up as a bad job,—begins to entertain sincere compassion for the Barings and their budget,—and finally entreats the family butler will be so very obliging as to cheat him on, in peace.

The butler, according to the superficial plausibilities of civilized life, though the booziest member of every establishment, is expected to be the most sober-looking. A peculiar decency of vesture and gesture is required of him. Something of the cut of a county member—something exceedingly square-toed and solemn,—is the complement extern most in vogue for the decanter of port.

In the households of bankers and professional men, a more dressy order of upper servant is preferred,—not only because he officiates in the double capacity of *valet de chambre*; but for the reason which induced the late Sir Charles C. to bestow badges upon his out-of-livery servants; because, having himself the air of a respectable upper servant, he was repeatedly required at his own balls to call up carriages, or bring shawls for fashionable ladies myopic enough to mistake him for his delegate.

But, though sober-looking as a judge, the butler should have a comely and portly aspect. He should look well-fed and un-careworn. There should be indication in his countenance that matters in his master house move upon castors;—that the weekly bills and refractory knife-cleaners are duly discharged; —and that everything like an impertinent rejoinder is as carefully bottled up as the Burgundy.

He must have an air of aptitude and decision, and a tone of authoritative good breeding. It is part of his business to take the guests out of the hands of the footmen, and deliver them in proper order to his master and mistress; tasks to be accomplished with the disdainful deference of a Lord Chamberlain.

It may be observed that the butler is almost always at daggers-drawn with his lady; who is sure to consider him a troublesome, officious personage,—apt to quarrel with the lady's maid for being too late at meals,—and to grudge the housekeeper her due allowance of sherry and ratafia for creams and jellies.

The footman is a slave more peculiarly her own. The footman accompanies the carriage, goes on errands, remembers addresses, conveys messages to tradespeople, and is more confided in, though a less confidential servant, than the butler. The footman has a thousand methods of judging of my lady's or the young ladies' loves and likings. He perceives in the daily drives *who* bows, *who* nods, *who* kisses hands,—*who* calls the carriage at Almack's or whispers as he hands Miss Julia into it, after the déjeuner or ball. John is able to announce a flirtation in the family to the housemaid, at least a fortnight before the butler drops a diplomatic hint to the housekeeper.

The butler is uniformly a Tory and a disciplinarian;—thumbs the John Bull on Sundays, and spells over the Times with one eye open, after his daily quart of stout. He has a sort of sullen and interested reliance in the immutability of the Church and the Corn Laws. Butlers, bishops, and landed proprietors he fancies to be as naturally affinitive as cart and horse. There may be horses without carts, he knows, but a cart can't move without a horse. No aristocracy secular or ecclesiastical,—no butlers! But this, it must be admitted, is mere livery logic and kitchen-stuff.

A butler is not the only public functionary who entertains an inordinate respect for property, as the true criterion of human merit; or who holds the only book worth speaking of to be a banker's. But his opinion on that point is very decided; and, so far from admitting that

Learning is better than house or land,

he respects the proprietor of a cowshed more than a senior wrangler or Seatonian prize-man. The three things he most detests to see at his master's table are, a bottle of the old Madeira he keeps for his private drinking, a poor relation, and an author. It puts him out of his calculations, indeed, to find every now and then a new novel announced by a Lady Clara, or a new poem by a Lord John; for he owns "he can't abide to hear of the nobility descending to such low-lived things."

There are, of course, as many classes of butlers in town and country, as there are of London men and country gentlemen. But it may suffice to consider two species of the genus: fierce extremes, such as the butler of Russell and the butler of Grosvenor

Squares,—"alike, but oh! how different!"—dissimilar in aspect and aspirations as a Guineaman and a Hindoo.

The butler of Russell Square is an obese, hazy-eyed personage, declining in years and in the corners of his mouth, sullen in disposition, yet to his superiors submissively spoken; having an eye to the main chance and to Mrs. Dobinson's prim-visaged lady's maid.

His master, Mr. Dobinson of Russell Square, is a thriving stockbroker, rich enough to be a prompt paymaster, and consequently to take the liberty of examining his own accounts; a sufficient pretext for his butler to regard him as a natural enemy, and to do his spiriting as ungently as Caliban.

Scrupulously punctual in the discharge of his duties, so as to escape jobation, Jobson takes a revengeful delight in the wry face which announces that a bottle of wine is corked; or when the man in authority, after finding fault with successive carving-knives, is forced to plead guilty to the toughness of the sirloin that smokes before him.

In his own principles of gastronomy, such a butler is a Pagan. He dresses the salad to be eaten at seven, early in the afternoon, and places it in a sunny window in company with the Sauterne and Moselle, which he is careful not to put into the wine-coolers till the last minute; and in the frostiest weather, leaves the claret to catch cold on a stone floor in a damp passage.

One of the great triumphs of his life is to pull in and out a silver watch, the size of Uncle Humphrey's clock, and announce, on the slightest retardment, that the cook is shamefully behind her time; while, should any unpunctuality on the part of Dobinson himself retard the usual dining-hour, Mr. Jobson issues his orders to "dish up," in a Stentorian voice, before the delinquent has time to give him his hat and gloves in the hall.—N.B. Be it observed that Jobson is as regularly mistered by the establishment as his master is Dobinsoned.

Fussy and consequential, his mode of bringing in the tea-things while the footman follows him with "the bubbling and loud hissing urn," is as authoritative as the air of the President of the Council; and there is a solid gravity in his mode of carrying round the fish-sauces at dinner, while the company are splitting their sides at some joke extracted from the last number of Punch, which cannot be too warmly applauded.

"Jobson is the steadiest man in the world,—Jobson is a man in whom I have implicit confidence," is Mr. Dobinson's continual certificate in favour of one whose voice is so sonorous at family prayers. Not the smallest peccadillo of the livery was he ever known to pass over. "I never heerd of such doings in a reg'lar establishmemt," is the grand arcanum of his form of government. The words "reg'lar establishment" have all the charm from *his* lips that the words "British Constitution" obtain in the ears of a Conservative constituency.

Next to opulence, he reverences "reg'-larity,"—or rather he accepts "reg'larity" as an indication of opulence. Most people well to do in the world are "reg'lar;"——fixed stars,—while your dashing, flashing, smashing meteors of fashionable life glitter for a moment, and are no more seen. Mr. Jobson would not have entered the service of a stockbroker,—stockbrokers being, like captains, "casual things,"—but that Dobinson had a very good character from his last butler, as being "the most reg'lar gentleman he ever lived with,—punctooal to a second." Without such a certificate, Mr. Jobson would not have taken him; and the butler has consequently a right to be displeased and mistrustful, when he finds the "punctooal" gentleman too late for dinner.

The butler himself being the most sedentary of created slaveys, has, of course, no indulgence for gadding. The coachman must drive to thrive, the footman flies to rise. But the family butler remains fixed in the family mansion from week's end to week's end, like a gold fish in its globe.

The utmost extent of air-taking in which he can indulge, is by keeping the street door open, with respectful deference, till the carriages of departing visitors have reached the angle of the square; the utmost stretch of sociability he is able to enjoy, consists in a game of cribbage with some brother butler of a next-door neighbour, when the Dobinsons dine out, or visit the theatre.

Even then, his companionability is of far from a cheerful nature. Habitual taciturnity has fixed its gripe upon him. His voice is modified so as to give short answers to his master, and long reprimands to the livery; and when Mr. Corkscrew, of No. 45, discusses with him a glass of stiff punch and the state of the times, he expands mechanically into murmurs; complains that Dobinson "is a prying fellow, as wants to do the gentleman," and "ministers shirkin' fellows as wants to do the people." Conviviality only renders him grumphier and grumphier. John or Thomas is gay in his small beer. But the butler remains sullen in his punch; fancying, perhaps, that a dogged humour is the nearest approach to sobriety.

A booziness, become almost constitutional, is his sole guarantee against committing himself by overt acts of ebriety. The man who is never quite sober, rarely becomes quite drunk. It is in vain that the Johns and Thomases who smart under his pragmatical jurisdiction, flatter themselves that, some day or other, Mr. Jobson and the coffee-tray will tumble together into the drawing-room, after a dinner party for which a dozen of wine has been decanted, with the usual butlerian diminutions. His accustomed minuet-step becomes only somewhat more of a *pas grave* for the wine he has swallowed; and their own transgressions lie as much exposed as ever to jobation, or rather, Jobson-ation.

"I should like to know, Thomas, when you ever saw *me* overtaken by liquor in a manner unbecoming a reg'lar family!" is still his cry; to say nothing of the more private lectures he bestows upon a young Cherubino of a Dobinsonian page, convicted of saying soft things to the under nursery-maid over the iron-spiked palings of the square; for Mr. J. "never *heerd* of such doings in a reg'lar family."

By dint of tears shed over family sermons on Sunday afternoons, and plausibility all the week and all the year round, Mr. Jobson gradually comes to be regarded as the Lord Angelo of family butlers. Dobinson himself stands in awe of his virtue and sobriety, —as a man "that wouldn't wrong his employers of a penny," or admit "an appetite rather to bread than stone."

Even when, one fine day, a faded, ragged, middle-aged woman brings to the area-gate a Jobsonian miniature, and when refused a trifling sum to furnish an apprentice-fee for the poor half-starved lad, is provoked into enlarging upon the backslidings of the highly respectable man in blue broadcloth and black silk stockings at a period when his round shoulders were graced with tags, and his silken hose were of white cotton, her charges are dismissed as frivolous and vexatious by Mrs. Dobinson's prim-visaged lady's-maid, and by Mrs. Dobinson's self.

In vain does the miserable woman produce duplicates of silver forks, alleged by the butler to have been lost by careless footmen; or silver spoons, for the disappearance of which suspicious kitchen-maids have been dismissed Dobinson has unlimited faith in his family butler. The vile-woman has evidently been suborned to belie him. Jobson is such an attached creature—Jobson is such an excellent man! It would be impossible for the household to go on "reg'larly" but for the superintendence of Jobson.

Jobson is consequently voted impeccable, and the wicked woman conveyed to the station-house. As certain bankers continue to be the most upright, honourable, and confidential men in the city, till the morning after the appearance of their names in the Gazette, so does the respectable butler continue to be respectable so long as he is able to keep his footing, and take thought what his master shall eat, what his master shall drink, and wherewithal he shall be clothed. The key-stone of the domestic arch, his services are indispensable to keep the family "reg'lar."

The butler of Grosvenor Square, on the other hand, provided there be neither house steward nor groom of the chambers over him to check his aspiring genius, is a more airy character than his eastern collaborator. Unless in archiepiscopal, episcopal, or very ancient Tory families of the aristocracy, elderly butlers, like old china, are out of date. Bonzes and josses went out with the Regency; and young servants and modern porcelain came in with Reform.

Even an old nurse is obsolete, unless in the form of a privy-councillor, a K.G.B., or a Welsh judge; and the fashionable butler is often on the sunny side of thirty; a man having too much regard for his complexion to infringe upon the wine-cellar, and too much interest in his own slimness to vulgarise on ale. An occasional glass of claret and sip of liqueur suffices the well-bred gentleman, who prides himself upon the graceful air with which he precedes the Marchioness, with noiseless step and unembarrassed respiration; and keeps his shape carefully within compass of that of his lord and master, so as to enable him to make suitable arrangements with his lordship's valet for his cast off wardrobe.

The Whittingham of Grosvenor Square would not be mistered for the world! Mister is, in fact, a name unfamiliar in "his lordship's establishment;" and the extremely gentlemanly gentleman, in Wellington boots or varnished pumps, who walks a-tiptoe, like Diomed, to announce his master's guests, would be disgusted to find himself thus conspicuously plebeianised.—"Ask Whittingham!" "Go to Whittingham!" carries with it a sort of confidential familiarity from the lips of his lovely lady, which makes him hold it more ennobling than the Guelphic order.

In lieu of the Times and John Bull, Whittingham reads the Morning Post and Court Journal; and is deeply versed in fashionable novels. In such a place as *his*, the porter being sole respondent at the door during her ladyship's absence, Whittingham having his afternoons to himself, divides them between his toilet, light literature, flirting with the French maid, compounding scandal with my lord's own man, and wondering how people can have the impertinence to send in bills, except at Christmas.

Not that he allows anything in the shape of a small account to molest his lord or lady. Whittingham knows better than to make himself disagreeable to his employers by appearing with a narrow slip of paper in his hand. Standing accounts, such as those of the Marquis, are, like the Marquis's peerage, of too old a date to be trifled with. No chance of percentage from *them*; and they are accordingly placed in a drawer in the hall-table till the end of the season, when the porter uses them to light his fires through the winter. It is only through the vulgar medium of the Post that claimants on a fashionable Marquis have a chance of obtaining attention between the month of January and the December next ensuing.

The Grosvenor Square butler is as tripsome in wit as in demeanour,—something of a conversation-man. All that is best of the *bon mots* of the clubs descends through *him* from his lordship's lips to the second table and he is careful to convey to my lady's woman the earliest intelligence of a clever debate, an interesting division, or a change of ministry.

Whittingham is almost as much a fixture, however, as Mr. Jobson. Saving that he has the use of his lordship's stall at the Opera during Ascot or Goodwood week, he indulges in no vulgar dissipations; and wonders, with an air of fastidiousness admirably copied from that of my lady, how people can show their face in the park.—A smart politician, Whittingham piques himself upon conservatism. He admits that "Melbourne is a gentlemanly fellow." But he cannot stand coalition with that vulgar brute, O'Connell, and abhors the word retrenchment. The fashionable world, *he* thinks, has been a lost case since the curtailment of the pension-list; and he sadly fears his Lord will live to rue the day he intrusted his proxy to a liberal administration.

Whittingham is too well bred to be on uneasy terms with any one residing under his lordship's roof.—But if an antipathy *could* ruffle the surface of so smooth a nature, it would, be against Florimond, the French cook.—He really cannot stand Monsieur Florimond. How is the subordination of the cellar to be kept up, with a cook who insists upon champagne to boil hams and stew kidneys,—Chably for his truffles and salmon,—and mulled claret for himself; besides cutting out the butler with Mademoiselle Amélie, and the stall at the Opera!—

Whittingham has no intention of growing grey or corpulent in service. Though the nature of his lordship's pursuits at Crockford's and Newmarket is such as to render the profits of his house unworthy mention, (unless a hundred a year from the wine-merchant, added to the butler's wages of seventy guineas, should be deemed sufficient to enable him to lay by for the benefit of younger children,) he has perfect reliance upon being properly provided for by my Lord.—A small place in the Household will be the very thing for him; something enabling him to wear ruffles and a sword by his side on gala days, as a fringe on the hem of royalty. As to the Customs, Excise, or Post-office, he would "beg to decline."—Whittingham has always been used to the society of gentlemen.

How different are these specimens of the family butler from the ancient serving-man of the old English gentleman,—the *bouteillier* or butler, who presided over the *paneterie*, or pantry; who bottled his master's sherrissack or Malvoisie for his master's drinking, instead of his own;—and brewed his master's ale, not only for his own drinking, but for the refreshment of all having claims on his master's hospitality;—who took genuine pride in the coals and blankets distributed to the poor;—wept tears of joy when an heir was born to the family, and tears of sorrow when its elders were borne to the grave. The heir was *his*,—the ale was *his*,—as one might guess by the tenderness with which he dealt with both.

His voice was never heard in chiding, then when some excess on the part of this master had brought on a fit of the gout,—or some imprudence on the part of his lady boded ill to her nurslings. With him, service was inheritance. He knew that the children to come after him would be dear to the children to come after his master; and for the general sake, as for the sake of conscience, his master's substance was sacred in his sight.

Such a butler was necessarily the head of a peaceable and well governed household. It is true he was a dunce. In *his* time, newspapers, daily or weekly, were unthumbed in the pantry; and, as to troubling himself about what was doing in the House, he regarded Parliament only as a solemn portion of Church and State, to be toasted at public dinners, and prayed for in parish churches, but not to be profaned by lips unclean.

But the wine he bottled was sounder, and the ale he brewed ripened more readily, than in these our times. In table-service, his attendance was impartial. He was not a bit more obsequious to Lord, the country neighbour, than to the needy hanger-on of the family; or, if a difference of assiduity *were* perceptible, it was simply in favour of the parson of the parish.

But, alas! "the gods are departing;" and stout old-fashioned serving-men seem also on the go. It is puzzling to decide what has become of them; whether they have gone into the reformed parliament, or the church, or the almshouse.—But, unless in the pages of Richardson or Steele, it is exceedingly difficult to meet with even the prototype of a comfortable FAMILY BUTLER.

The French Cook

THE NAME OF FRENCH COOK conveys to the popular mind the image of a lean and shrivelled individual in a white nightcap and apron, speaking broken English, and inflicting broken meat, frogs, and other filthiness, upon the Earl, his master, at the rate of three or four hundred guineas per annum.

The French cook, in the highest sense of the word, is a well-dressed, well-mannered gentleman, who stands behind her Majesty's or his Grace's chair during dinner, stirring a smoking sauce in a silver tureen; after having appeared for an hour in the kitchen before dinner, with a napkin under his chin, and a gold spoon in his hand, to taste and pronounce upon the gravies and other condiments prepared by his subordinates, according to his manifesto of the early morn.

Such a man was Carême, such Ude, such Francatelli; such, doubtless, the Vatel, whose name is as immortal in the records of gastronomic art, as that of Racine or Molière in the dramatic.

An artist of this description is an individual not to be lightly treated of; a cook of this description is a distinguished man. It is, only in England that he is degraded by the antediluvian name of cook. In France he is called the CHEF, like the head of any other department,—"*chef de bureau*,"—"*chef d'escadron*,"—"*chef d'opéra*,"—"*chef de cuisine*." In England, the only chief we recognise is the Commander of her Majesty's armies at the Horse Guards; and to talk of the chief of the kitchen would have a Mohican or Narraganseth sound, savouring of the wigwam.

Nevertheless, there is something ennobling in the word. "Tell the cook," or "tell the *chef*," are as different as prose and poetry. A mere "cook" would never have worn point ruffles, or fallen on the point of his sword, like the great Vatel; or have lost his place in the royal kitchen from an over-sensitive temperament, like the Francatelli of the present day. We have little doubt that the honourable distinctions conveyed in the word "*chef*," have engendered more capital *entrées* than the pages of Brillat, Savarin, or Grimod de la Reynière.

The English are notoriously the most backward of civilized nations in the art of cookery. The profession does not obtain sufficient honour in Great Britain. We treat a great artist of the gastronomic department, as we would treat any other menial, without reflecting that a first-rate cook must be a man of genius; a man combining the inventive and combinative faculties in no ordinary degree; a man of almost poetical temperament, yet of prompt judgment, and untirable activity of body and mind.

Such advantages do not occur united half-a-dozen times in a century. A Carême is as rare as a Malibran, a Taglioni, a Rossini. The rejoinder, which has been successively assigned to a score of men of genius in the course of the last five hundred years, from Hans Holbein to Pacchierotti, when "sprighted" by some saucy lordling with messages from Court, "Tell the King, your master, that he may make a dozen nobles by the breath of his mouth, but that there is but one Holbein," might very properly be reiterated by certain modern *chefs*, who have been treated as lightly, or rather heavily, in royal households, as if any other member thereof were capable of corn-pounding *a bisque d'e'écrévisses*!

The consequence of this disparagement is that the greatest cooks of the age prefer almost any foreign service to that of an English family. The good and great refrain from our shores, and the cheap and nasty inundate our contaminated kitchens. Secure in our almost savage ignorance of the principles of his art, the *trousse-poulet*, or scullion of a French establishment makes his appearance in London, in a velvet waistcoat and gilt guard-chain, with a certificate bearing the name of a Russian prince, purchased for half-a-crown of an *écrivain publique*; on the strength of which, he is instantly engaged, at a salary of a hundred guineas a year, (instead of the kicks and broken victuals he has been receiving for wages at some eating-house on the Boulevards) to poison the frequenters of some fashionable club or coffee-house; who, in their disgust at his villanous performances, fall back upon the everlasting joint or boiled fowl of their ancestors, and go roast-beefing and plum-pudding it in their graves.

John Bull is never weary of declaring that he detests "kickshaws," *i.e.*, the "*quelques choses*," by which French scullions generalize the hard names of the *entrées* they presume to murder; because he possesses in his national bill of fare two or three dishes of unequalled merit,—the lordly haunch of venison, the sirloin of beef, the saddle of mutton, the green goose, to say nothing of turtle in all its savoury varieties,—viands excellent after their kind, for the ravenous maw of a debater or a fox-hunter.

But it is by this blind and positive rejection of alimentary civilization, that London perpetuates the unwholesome crudities of its kitchen. *Probatio est.* Is there a capital under the sun that groans louder under the torture of its indigestions?—Is there, a population that insults the eyes of Europe more revoltingly by its advertisements of aperitives?

Roast mutton and apple-pie are in fact a matter of necessity in our cookless country; and our self-love is glad to make a virtue of necessity. Charcoal is a costly thing in our diminutive and deforested island. We dine without soup, because we know not how to make it, except as an article of luxury; and prefer an unsightly chop to a savoury cutlet, simply because the chop is most come-at-able. But it puts a fair face on the nakedness of the land to affect a contempt for "kickshaws."

That the "plain roast and boiled," in which we pretend to delight, are, in truth, anything but delightful, may be attested by the multiplicity of Chili vinegar and Cayenne pepper, soys, ketchups, sauces, King of Oude's, Harvey's, Reading, Lopresti's, and other British compounds, with whose astringent juices we vitrify the coats of our stomachs, to enable them to retain our daily rations of tasteless fish, flesh, and fowl, instead of having them suitably prepared for table.

The plainest of our plain cooks cannot suffer a poor innocent chicken to come to table without deluging it in parsley and butter; and fennel sauce, or melted butter tasting of smoke and the flour-tub, fill our sauce-boats with eternal shame, and prove us to be only advanced a stage beyond the savageness of our hip-haw-and-acorn-cramming forefathers.

Of all cooking animals, in short, the Englishman is by intuition the least expert, and by indocility, the least improvable. An exotic master is indispensable in order to subdue his natural tendency to exaggeration, and soften the insensitive harshness of the northern palate.

Still, this is not matter for despair. Twenty years ago, when the Horticultural Society was not, our gardens were reduced to an humble show of mignionette, scarlet lychnis, and ten-weeks' stocks, instead of the brilliant sprinkling of calceolarias, pelargoniums, and coreopses, which now brighten the parterre. Twenty years ago, when the Zoological Society was not, our juveniles knew not, save by effigy, to distinguish a bison from a tapir; and believed in the existence of the cameleopard, as we believe in the Apocalypse—by faith. And why may not the perceptions of a succeeding generation be improved as regards the flesh-pots of Great Britain, by the establishment of a Gastronomic Society? For one man who cares to look at a pied, pheasant, there are ten thousand who love a well-roasted one; and in the opinion of the many, not all the orchideous plants or rose-bushes lectured upon by Professor Lindley, vie in importance with the naturalization of a single edible root or leguminous novelty. Say, excellent John Bull! a new hyacinth, or a new potato?—"Speak, or die!" Why, an' thou speak the truth, thou wouldst not give a potato for a whole wilderness ot'hyacinths!

It is easy for the great ones of Great Britain, rejoicing in their three courses and dessert prepared by a French cook, English roaster, and Italian confectioner,—assert, and with truth, that better dinners are given in London than in any capital in Europe. With Romney Marsh, the South Downs, and our domestic parks

for pastures,—with the circumjacent sea for our fish course,—
and the colonies for our spice-box,—how can it be otherwise?
But the greatest number, whose happiness, social and political,
has at length become a matter of consideration,—the greatest
number, who are compelled, by the plainness of their cooks,
to a daily diet of crude meat, tasteless vegetables, and doughy
pastry,—to tough and scorched chops, with the indigestible
horrors of an apple dumpling,—are deeply interested in the
promotion of a science which, by making tender the food of
man, in the sequel makes tender his heart. We conscientiously
believe that half the obdurate parents and brutal husbands of
middle life, are produced by the cold meat and pickles of their
anti-gastrophilic propensities.

Let the education committees look to it! It were a far more
philosophical exercise of humanity to enable "the foolish fat
scullions" of this ill-fed empire, to compound good wholesome
soup out of a modicum of meat and vegetables, and to give to the
universal potato salt, savour, and digestibility by the simplest of
processes, than perplex them by rules of arithmetic, or superfluous
delicacy of orthography.

It is disgusting to think in what Hottentot ignorance these
poor creatures are at present reared for a calling which, properly
refined and appreciated, enables a mere mortal to provide a
banquet worthy of the gods. Among *us* a cook is as unconscious
of the sacredness of his or her calling, as if they were no higher
in the scale of domestic life than a burnisher of plate, or sweeper
of cobwebs. But between a footman or house maid, and the
individual whose good or evil service influences the health and
comfort, nay, prolongs or curtails the life of the family, how vast
a step!

The neglect or malefactions of the cook may injure the
innermost man of the most illustrious,—whether his or her
master, or the guest of his or her master; and the errors of a
Chancery judgment, or a break down in parliament, have been
caused before now by the half-raw vegetables of a spring soup, or
the crudity of an ill-boiled cod's head and shoulders;—a matter of
serious consideration for the legislative wisdom of the country.

In the education of the French *chef*, on the contrary, a thousand fortuitous advantages combine. If less catechised or belaboured with the rule of three than our unhappy youths in crumpet-caps and yellow worsted stockings, the French starveling who is father to the French cook, is schooled from his earliest childhood in the mysteries of the fine-arts, by admittance gratis to all the public exhibitions, and a variety of courses of public lectures. At the Louvre, his eye becomes habituated to the glorious forms of antiquity: and even if too idle to attend the public School of Design, he grows insensibly impressed by harmonies of shape and colour. On public festivals, he is admitted gratis to the theatres; and at the opera, acquires a taste for music, dancing, and the classics. His tone of mind becomes gradually refined, his powers of invention awakened.

His daily lounge is the Palais Royal; where, at the provision shops of Chevet or Corcellet, he gazes upon the Perigord pie, the truffled turkey, the *poularde* delicate as the cheek of beauty; the glistening carp, the speckled salmon-trout, the ferocious lobster, the picturesque roebuck, the tender asparagus, the melting ortolan, the rosy teal, the red-legged partridge, the luxurious mullet; with an endless cornucopia of figs, dates, oranges, and pine-apples, standing among stores of olives, capons, and the crisp white *nougat* of the sweet south.

As the sculptor foresees his *chef d'ceuvre* in the shapeless block of marble, the future *chef* foresavours his courses in this gastronomic medley. In the windows of Véfour, Véry, the *Frères Provençaux*, the Café de Perigord, he notes and criticises their buffet of *paté de foie gras*, cray-fish, Brittany butter, cutlets of *pré salé* crumbed for the fire,—larks marshalled on their little silver spits,—or *beccafichi*, rolled in their vine-leaves.

There does he pause and ponder! There do the thick-coming fancies of genius in spire his mind! There is nothing nearer akin to a great poet, than a great gastronomer: their faculties of invention being destined to promote the happiness of the million, while themselves are a-hungered or in despair. We are inclined to place the creators of a *supréme de volaille*, and of Paradise Lost, in nearly the same category of exalted beings.

And is such a man as this to be abased to the menialities of the servants' hall, or even of the steward's room? In France, the royal *chef, porte l'épée au côte*, and is a man of honour. In England, the Queen's *maître d'hotel*, who is also head cook, wears an official carving-knife. Such weapons should be chivalrously sacred!—The Board of Green Cloth has no right to deal with them as with the vulgar throng of lackey kind.—The Board of Green Cloth should recal to mind the cruel destinies of Correggio, the most exquisite of painters, weighed down by royal humiliation unto the grave.

In France, the memory of *le grand Vatel* is as familiarly talked of as "*le grand Sully,*" or "*Louis le Grand.*" The story of the said great Vatel is pretty well known among us. Nevertheless the last English translation of Madame de Sévigné's letters gives so *ignorantissimé* a version of the matter as to deserve comment.

Vatel was cook to the Prince de Condé; and on the intimation of Louis the Fourteenth that the Court would spend a few days with his trusty and well-beloved cousin at his palace of Chantilly, twenty' miles from Paris, the great man read in the announcement of this royal visit his brevet of immortality.

To Chantilly, accordingly, repaired the Court; and though his Majesty was observed to eat, drink, and sleep there during the first four-and-twenty hours entirely to his royal satisfaction, the tender honour of Vatel was wounded to the quick on perceiving that, at the first day's dinner, the first course was second-rate; and that at the table of the ladies of honour, two roasts were deficient!

The unfortunate *chef* slept not that fatal night! It was in vain that the chamberlain of the Prince de Condé as well as the comptroller of the King's household, assured him nothing could be more admirable than his arrangements—nothing more exquisite than his *entrées*;—that the King had eaten with appetite, and praised with dignity. The sensitive Vatel wrung his hands, and refused to be comforted!—Two roasts had been wanting!

By daybreak he was at his post,—inspecting the progress of preparations for the royal breakfast. But with a countenance expressive of bitter anguish and unsolaceable remorse, he was heard to inquire repeatedly of the clerk of the kitchen and his legion of myrmidons, or *marmitons*, whether "the *marée* had arrived?"

"The *marée*?" quoth the English translator; "what on earth is the *marée*?"—and turning to the dictionary, finds that marée bears the interpretation of "tide—flux and reflux of the sea." Scarcely conceiving it possible that the flux and reflux of the sea could, have been expected by the night-coach at Chantilly, he consequently gravely assures us that Vatel was heard inquiring on all sides whether " the *salt water* were arrived!"

His subordinates," continues our translator, "answered him in the affirmative, and showed him a small portion of salt water, forwarded from Dieppe, without being aware that a similar quantity of salt water was to be forwarded from each of the fishing towns of La Manche."

The agonized *chef* was now reduced to despair; under the influence of which, as it is only too well known, he retired to his own chamber, exclaiming that his honour was irretrievably tarnished,—fell upon his sword,—and EXPIRED!—

And all this, according to our English translation of the works of Sévigné, for the sake of a little "salt water!"—"*Et voilà comme on écrit l'histoire!*"

It need not, of course, be suggested to our accomplished readers, that *marée* is the general designation of fish, according to the idiom of the kitchen. It was fast-day ; and Vatel, conceiving himself condemned to a wretched brill and a few whitings, instead of the miraculous draught of turbots and mullets on which he had foreseen occasion to exercise his art, unwilling to survive his humiliation, precipitated himself out of the "frying-pan into the fire," and became immortal as Encelades!—

This was a fault. This was dying like Correggio, or dying like Keats. It may have been great for a great cook to fall at the instigation of wounded honour; but it would have been greater to have lived and extended the buckler, or saucepan cover of genius, over his scars.

Carême, Ude, nay, even Francatelli, would have rushed to the *piscinium* of Chantilly; and, snatching forth its grey carp, voracious pike, or speckled trout, converted *them* into turbots and lobster sauce. Nay, we are by no means certain that one, at least, of the three would not have made a sweetbread figure to perfection as a dish of mullets *en papillote*; or caused a turkey poult to assume the form of a cod's head and shoulders!

But in the times of Louis le Grand the science was in its infancy. Substitutes and *ambigus* were not; and Vatel lost his life for a turbot.

By the way, though the science of the *casserole* was in its leading strings, we very much doubt whether that of the confectioner were not then at years of discretion. The long minority of Louis the Fourteenth probably rendered the cultivation of the art of confection the most delicate courtiership of the epoch, as at the present day in Madrid.

From his infancy to his old age, Louis was addicted to *bonbons*; and the fêtes given upon his marriage,—when a temple of love was erected in the centre of the royal gardens, to which there was access by four avenues of exquisite trees, the abundant fruits pendent whereon were preserved, or candied, or *fac-similes* of sugar, producing, by the light of thousands of lamps glaring among the leaves, a more than magical effect,—have found no rivalship in modern times. But alas! between Colbert the gorgeous, and Guizot the prudential, there exists the unfathomable gulf produced by a couple of revolutions!

To return to our cooks—(for from the ridiculous to the sublime there is but a paragraph!)—to return from cabinet ministers to cooks, the French cook, as he exists in England, is usually some ambitious man, some Thiers of the frying pan, who, with a view to his own aggrandizement and expansion from *sous-chef*, expatriates himself, and submits to become smoke-dried as a rein-deer's tongue, as well as to be divorced from his beloved opera, and *Boulevards*.

Arrived in London, he is enchanted with all he beholds. The shops of Grove, of Fortnum, of Giblett, of Fisher, fill his soul with new conceptions of the good things of this world. All sorts and conditions of edibles seem prepared for his hand. It appears only necessary to exclaim,

Fire burn, and caldron bubble,

for Fentum's stoves to convert a well-filled larder into a capital dinner.

By degrees, however, the enthusiasm of the new comer declines; for he finds that he begets no enthusiasm in return. The influence of the climate is oppressive to his faculties, while the gross ignorance of his master humiliates his wounded feelings. He is unappreciated, unpraised, unrewarded,—save by his salary. The unpunctuality of the English is martyrdom to a cook of genius. He provides a hot dinner for half-past seven, to be eaten cold at half-past eight. His *soufflés* fall heavy on his soul. His viands lose their flavour, their elasticity, their complexion; and if souls so magnanimous as that of Vatel still existed in the regions of the spit, there would probably be half a dozen inquests per season, upon gentlemen of his calling, wounded in their sense of honour by the failure of their dinners.

In half the best English houses, the *entrées* are mere matters of show; and the simple roaster stands accordingly higher in the favour of his master, than the most accomplished cook. Even when eaten, they are misunderstood. The influence of our climate, and the early use of the fiery wines of the Peninsula, produce a serious injury to the palate. While still in our non-age, Cayenne pepper, Chili vinegar, and soy, have sapped the very foundations of our gastronomic morality. For the palate of the *gourmand* may become as *blasé* as the soul of a *roué*.

It is for the depraved appetites of such men, that the French cook has to play his fantastic tricks;—to devil chickens, and pepper partridges,—nay, to pepper woodcocks!—The pure and transparent gravies of France are insufficient to provoke the jaded appetites of those who have begun life with curry, or a dressed wild duck. By the time a French cook has been three seasons in London, his principles are subverted. He no longer knows how to distinguish right from wrong. His chief business is to make his dinner look well on the table.

His life in the household, meanwhile, is a wretched one. He finds himself an object of universal mistrust. "Those wretches of foreigners," or "that cursed French fellow," are terms which resound daily in his ears; and he is unluckily a better linguist than the translator of Madame de Sévigné.

Since the Courvoisierian catastrophe, this evil has increased. But from time immemorial, the French cook has been as much a matter of disgust in every aristocratic establishment, as the royal confessor in the days of the Stuarts. The vulgar mind of Great Britain is imbued with prejudices, and delights in perversion. The servants' hall is sure to call every foreigner a spy, and a Jesuit; though what is purported by the charge, it would be sorely puzzled to explain. While the hapless tosser-up of omelets is as guiltless of religion or politics as a New Zealander, they hate him, because he is "outlandish,"—because "Wellington beat the French at Waterloo;"—or, in point of fact, because the French beat the English over a charcoal fire, as thoroughly as the English the French by the fire that produces another kind of stew, and is characteristic of another order of broil.

The French cook is, in short, the Pariah of the household. Unless the diamond shirt-studs and varnished boots in which he sallies forth to the Opera have captivated the heart of the under housemaid, not a creature under his master's roof but regards him as a species of evil spirit,—a man who would poison for hire, if he did not receive higher wages as a *chef de cuisine*.

The only houses where these unfortunate individuals obtain any ascendency are the clubs and hotels. *There* their activity, their adroitness, their powers of combination, become invaluable. Aboriginal men-cooks of some excellence are to be met with in such establishments; but it is now recognised that, though we produce general officers, the field-marshal of a first-rate kitchen *must* be of Gallic blood, and born with pretensions to the *cordon bleu*.

But it is also in such establishments they presume furthest upon the unsusceptibility of an English palate. There is an anecdote on record, that the inestimable *chef* of one of the first London coffee-houses,—nay, the very first,—once bargained, day after day, with a celebrated Bond Street fishmonger, for a turbot which, at the close of the week, became "a filthy bargain."

Still the artist persisted in inquiring after that "dom foine feesh!"

"It is good for nothing now," replied the fishmonger. Well, if you trow him away, give him to *me*."

"Willingly," said the good-humoured tradesman, "on condition that you tell me what you intend to do with it."

"*Ma foi*, I make him a sauce twice as nashty as himself, and de foine shentlemen vill call him *dom* foine!"

Let it not be supposed that the *chef* was to blame in this. If he had not found hundreds of customers prepared to be made fools of, he would not have attempted to make them fools.

The virtues of the French cook are sobriety, activity, and zeal. A first-rate artiste is supported in the discharge of his duties by his own *amour-propre*. He glories in his calling, and feeling capable of providing the nectar and ambrosia of the gods, turns with loathing from the vulgar potables of London. He is never tired, never sullen;—passionate, and tyrannical with, his *subs.*, like most great potentates,—but never sullen. Ude is said to have boasted that but one Ude and one Napoleon adorn a century,—probably from inward consciousness of affinity between the genius of the two.

But, though by vocation tyrants, great cooks seldom arise under the dominion of great despots. It is under the sway of *les rois fainéans*, that the stewpan is seen to flourish. Under George IV. and Louis XVIII. gigantic strides were made in the science of gastronomy; under Napoleon and Louis Philippe, reckless bolters of their food, cookery loses a cubit of her stature; while, under Victoria, the anything but *fainéante* Queen, Francatelli, the Coriolanus of Pimlico, was banished the royal kitchen!

It would not much surprise us if, in the sequel of these reforming times, the white nightcap should be altogether Joseph Humed out of the palace gates; and some hideous Mrs. Glasse, or detestable Mrs. Rundell, be found presiding over the *ragoûts* of Majesty. As sure as two and two make four, future travellers will come to the stately furnaces and stoves of Windsor Castle, and cry aloud,—"Where is the French cook?" and echo will reply, in a plaintive voice,—"*Where* is the FRENCH COOK!"

The Body-Coachman

A STATE-COACHMAN IS ONE of the most prominent embodyings of the national character that presents itself to the naked eye in the metropolis.

John Bull, as formerly typified,—John Bull,—portly, rubicund, spruce, yet easy in his garments,—jovial yet sober enough to avoid running against a post,—mulish, and apt to resent upon the animals under his lash, the wiggings he receives from his master or missus,—John Bull is scarcely to be met with at this present writing, in this land of anti-corn-law associations, unless seated in state upon a laced hammercloth.

With lustrous, rosy, and whiskerless face, round as a Nonsuch apple,—a Falstaff in livery,—a waist beyond all bounds and a pair of calves such as might belong to the dun cow of the Earl of Warwick,—the state-coachman of Majesty or the Lord Mayor, often boasts a presence whose dignity might become the woolsack. We do not mean profanely to compare these heads of the coaching department with the speakers of the Upper House; or to opine how far in either case the wisdom may reside in the wig. But we confess that if, according to a great authority, "Kings themselves are only ceremonies," we are apt to fall into the error of regarding Lord Chancellors and State Coachmen as a main portion of the pomp and circumstance of the British constitution.

In one respect, the assimilation holds especially good. No man is pre-ordained for a Chancellor or a State Coachman. Lesser men are born great. But the greatness of *these* great men,—that is, the greatness of one of them, and the bigness of the other,—is an achievement of their own. The body-coachman, like the Chancellor, is *fils de ses œuvres*. The works of the one consisting in stuffing,—the other in cramming. The one imbibes ale,—the other Hale; and between repletion of body and fulness of knowledge, both swell into public distinction.

It is worthy of Dogberry to assert that reading and writing come by nature, but that to be a personable man is the gift of Providence. The same dispensation that gives to the body-coachman the abdominal protuberance becoming his box,—assigns to the lawyer the crooked and crannyfied brain, qualifying him for the torture of the witness-box.

A thin coachman is as anomalous an object in nature, as a dwarf generalissimo, or a thick rope-dancer. Unless his face be labelled to serve as a certificate of the merit of his master's home-brewed, and his figure emulate the form of the butt that contains it, he is unworthy of his cloth,—*i.e.* his hammercloth. The state-coachman should be a man above the world, in other respects besides his coach-box; care-proof, and inaccessible to all diseases save gout or dropsy. He should be high as the monument, and solid as St. Paul's.

It is clear, therefore, that such a vocation announces at once one of the happiest and best of mankind. The same qualities that ought to recommend a man to the attention of a chapter, in a *congé d'élire*, must clearly influence every discreet nobleman in the choice of a body-coachman. Though like other blades valued for temper and sharpness, his real excellence consists in the almost holy serenity of soul which causes his face to shine like that of the sun in an almanack; and the crimson doublet buttoned over his paunch, to resemble a well-stuffed red velvet ottoman, bordered with gold.

A remarkable transition in the history of coaching life, was that which metamorphosed a certain Joe Tims, from being shoe-black to a preparatory school, into the twenty-stone Jehu of the beautiful Countess of ——; he, whose snowy wig at the last drawing-room emulated the snow-clad summit of Mont Blanc;

and whose goodly legs describe the segment of an ellipsis whereof the bases are never less than two feet asunder.

The Durham ox, seated on a hammercloth upon its beam-ends, arrayed in a livery by Stulz, would scarcely display a more substantial form and pressure. If, as it is asserted, the state-coachman of the Emperor of Russia must be always a general, our friend, Joe Tims—we ask pardon, *Mister* Tims—clearly deserves to be field-marshal!

Who could have thought it!—I never look down upon him from my attic window as the natty *vis-à-vis* of her ladyship bowls along the street, with its lustrous panels and aristocratic decorations, its pair of noble horses before, full of spirit, action, and blood, and its pair of ignoble asses behind, all tags and lace, subjection and sauciness, with Tims, square and pompous, on his flowing hammercloth, with Atlantean shoulders, and toes pointed East and West,—like Old Spain, with a footing in either hemisphere,—without recalling to mind the little red-headed scamp whose *summum bonum* of youthful happiness was to gnaw a raw turnip on a gate-post!

Yet let it not be supposed that Tims's ascent from *that* post to his present was by a hop, skip, and jump. "Oh! who can tell how hard it is to climb" to the lofty prominence of a box of any distinction!—"There are two ways," says the sage, "of attaining the apex of a pyramid,—that of the eagle, who stoops to it from the skies,—that of the reptile, who crawls up to it from the earth." Let the judgment of the public decide upon Joe Tims's mode of achieving Jehudicial greatness.

Marvellous was the ugliness of the boy Tims, father to the man Tims, at twelve years old: that is, not so much the ugliness as the diminutiveness. Those who wished to investigate his pigmy features felt disposed to promote him to the point of a needle; not as one of the dancing angels described by casuists, but in order to insert him under the reflection of a microscope. He was an orphan, charity fed; and we all know how the parochial "charity that feedeth the hungry" feedeth orphans. If the Providence that nourishes the young ravens be equally sparing in their diet, it may account for the rarity of old ravens in the ornithological world.

Joe was, in short, kept as near the boundaries of starvation as might set at nought a verdict of infanticide; and he might have been weighed in the balance against a full-grown barn-door fowl (*not* fed on charity), and found wanting. The little fellow, however was born for future greatness—or bigness; and lived on, as a boy of ten, despite of beadle and churchwardens.

It was while awaiting his apprenticeship that Joe became henchman to seventy other boys, nearly as ragged and as hungry as himself. He was what is called to "work for his victuals" till the chimney-sweeper had a vacancy; and these victuals were of even a lower nature than those commonly called "broken." They might have been called "smashed;"—for potatoe-peelings and egg-shells had their share in the hell-broth brewed for the parish-boy.

At length Joe Tims did what any other sensible young man would have done in the same situation—he ran away. Hunger is said to eat through stone-walls. Hunger ate through the patience of poor Joe, leaving him nothing to eat in return. But though it be proverbially said, that "he who runs may read," it does not follow that he who runs may eat. All that Joe Tims got by running was, thinner than ever.

Arrived in the great Babylon, Joe Tims followed the example of Wisdom, and cried in the streets; and, as in the case of Wisdom, "no man regarded." Those who, seeing him seated on a door-step, with his exiguous frame manifested through the fissures of his garments, learned on interrogating the truant that he was "an unfortunate lad out of place," thought him very much out of place indeed; and bestowed upon him the gratuity proverbially said to be the allowance of a race to which, it must be admitted, he bore a strong family resemblance.

The wretched little morsel soon found that a place was as hard to find for a run away parish apprentice, as for a sucking politician unbacked by parliamentary interest. Fair ladies do not, like Boz or Paul de Koch, take their pages from the streets. Even the small genteel families in want of an odd boy to clean knives, seemed to consider little Joe a great deal too odd for them. After a week's experience as a gutterling of the fashionable world, poor Tims began to remember yearningly, not the flesh-pots of Israel—

for flesh-pots he had never seen—but the broth of eggshells and potatoe-peelings, simmering so appetizingly over the kitchen-fire of the preparatory school!

There was very little left of the poor orphan but the bones, when one day a walking apothecary, much resembling him whom the facetiousness of managers usually causes to embody the outline of the needy poison-selling wretch drawn by Shakspeare in his Romeo, struck by the meagreness of the child, and perhaps conceiving that before long he might afford without much trouble of preparation a pleasing addition to his anatomical museum, proceeded to engage him as scrub; to carry about the oil-skin covered basket, the Pandora's box, from which magnesia and rhubarb flew out daily, to the great detriment of the invalided portion of society; leaving a small account, not like, Hope, but Despair, at the bottom!—Pills above,—bills below.—

Joe was enraptured. The sight of jars and phials in the apothecary's shop conveyed a vague idea of food; and though, on finding that the gallipots contained only leeches and electuaries, and the phials cathartics, the charming illusion vanished from his mind, the bare imagination of a feast had done something to restore his courage.

Besides, his body was no longer as bare as his imagination. Mr. Senna, afraid perhaps of generating the cholera in his household by exposing that exiguous frame at the same moment to cold and hunger, had cut down one of his own threadbare suits into a covering for Joe;—cut it down, *bien entendu*, as the victims of the law are cut down, when all is over with them. Threadbare, however, as was the cloth, it served him as it does the gentlemen in black when quarrelsome in their natures,—as a protection.

For those who, like a royal bulletin, are fond of "progressive improvement," it is a good thing to begin where Joe Tims began, in the lowest mud wherein human clay may be compelled to roll. Every step in life taken by the orphan was necessarily an advancement. The household of Mr. and Mrs. Senna, from which so many home-reared errand-boys had fled in dismay, appeared to poor Joe a land of Canaan, overflowing with milk and honey.

Though, like a lady's album, fed with scraps, the fare appeared to *him* more luxurious than the venison and turtle of the Egyptian Hall on Lord Mayor's Day. It was curious to see how his slender limbs now began, like Hermione, to "round apace." The conversion of one of Pharoah's lean kine into one of his fat ones, could not have presented a more curious contrast. Mr. Senna's opposite neighbour, the parish clerk, who took in day-scholars, and understood the difficulty of keeping boys in their teens sleek and well looking, was heard to whisper to a brother-scholar of the ferule, that the apothecary's errand-boy, like Mithridates, seemed to possess the art of fattening upon drugs.

Luck, which impertinent people have defined as the providence of fools, soon threw the dapper little errand-boy in the way of preferment. One of Senna's professional avocations consisted in courting the mews adjoining his dispensary. Not that he administered to man *and* beast; those who were beastly enough to swallow his medicines being invariably bipeds. But he was a great man among coachmen's wives, labouring with small families; and not a parlour on the first floor over the stables, but had its chimney-piece adorned with his labelled bottles.

It follows that, even as the boys of Dr. Caius followed their master to the field, the boy of Dr. Senna followed *his* to the rack and manger. By dint of carrying jalap and ginger to the little centaurs, Joe began to imbibe a taste for horseflesh. He had commenced life by longing after a stalled ox, and was now beginning to cast eyes of covetousness upon stalled horses; the only provender which troubled his imagination being that which disturbed the mind of Nick Bottom, in the arms of Titania—*viz.,* a sieve of corn, and a truss of good tender hay. He was always getting chidden by old Senna for mews-ing away his time; was apt to whistle while rubbing down ostlerwise his master's counter; and to exclaim "Wo ho!" to the still, instead of extracting the funnel, and suspending its operations.

One morning when, following his Houhnyhm propensities, he was as usual loitering near a stable-door, instead of proceeding with his oil-skin basket up the ladder leading to the state some body-coachman, a certain Captain Flashdragon, who had repaired to the fountainhead, or trough-head of coachmanship, to look out for a tiger for his cab, seized him by the shoulder, and inquired whether he knew anything of horses?

A *parvenue* ladyship of the West-end, startled by an inquiry whether she knew anything of the Patronesses of Almacks, could not have replied more deprecatingly that he "had not much the honour of their acquaintance; but that he was most anxious to improve it."

Captain Flashdragon's next interrogatory: was of a still more alarming character, And pray, my fine fellow, how would you like to be a tiger?"

Joe Tims had often been accused in earlier days of being a wolf. It had never entered into his calculations to progress into a tiger.

The nature and attributes of tigerism, however, as set forth by the gallant captain, were far from unsatisfactory. Joe, who possessed instincts of almost feline cleanliness, and whose very soul had rebelled against the filthy rags of his kittenhood, was sorely tempted by the description of the pair of snow-white tights, tops, and gloves, awaiting the legitimate tiger of a Captain Flashdragon. The natty dark-blue livery, with its short divergent skirts almost rivalling those of a beef-eater or fireman, completed the charm; and lo! he was induced to request the compounder of medicines would "provide himself," and to place himself under the measures of the captain's compounder of liveries.

In enumerating the advantages attached to the tigerhood of his establishment, the Captain had, of course, omitted to state that the fifteen guineas per annum were paid septennially; and that though the wages he gave were merely nominal, the cuffs were *not*. The tenderest plateful ever served at the Steaks could not have been more strenuously belaboured with the rolling-pin, than the flesh of poor Joe after jogging for a season at the rear of Flashdragon's cab.

A more demoralizing service could not have been found for the poor little bottle imp, than that of a broken-down man about town, in times when policemen were not, and when the magistracy regarded rouge et noir as a legitimate recreation. But for a native simplicity of character, such as we have already described as leading exclusively to the wig Episcopal and Jehu-dicial, it would soon have been all dickey with the virtues of Joe!

But the cat-like cleanliness of his inward man was equal to that of his outward. From a boy, he had been able to touch pitch—and even pitch and toss—without being defiled, and when at length Flashdragon bolted for Boulogne, leaving his cab and tiger at the mercy of society, no matter whether the Mendicity or the Zoological, Tim was still the same blameless individual who had eked out his early subsistence with sloes and crabs,—and at Senna's sweetened his dry bread with electuary, as with raspberry jam!

What a destiny.—At fifteen, on the wide world, without friends and without a character!

For once, the stature of Joe Tims stood him in stead. He was too slight to be worth pressing into a gang of housebreakers, and too tall to be shoved in through a pane of glass. He was therefore allowed to starve on, untempted.

Instinct carried him back to the Sennatorial mews, in quest of employment; when lo! the first news that greeted him was, that at the close of an "unprecedently season," (as the theatres have it,) his quondam master was setting up a gig, which the *mews*ical families under his pestle and mortar did not fail to denominate "old Senna's influenza gig."

A gig supposes a horse,—a horse, a groom; and poor Joe, sorely out of employ, and consequently out at elbows, judged it better to become once more the Lancelot Gobbo of the Old Jew. Senna was well satisfied to take him back. Joe could find his way blindfold to all his master's old patients. As mechanically as an undertaker's horse paces to the churchyard, could Tims impel the influenza gig to the doors of all the rheumatic spinsters and hypochondriac widows in the vicinity. At first, indeed, the apothecary, fired with the ambition of declaring "*l'état c'est moi!*" took it into his head to handle the ribands and brandish the whip. But a certain coachmaker's bill, the result of this wild exploit, reduced him to reason and a compound fracture at the same time; and it appeared to be no small relief to him to discover that "Cap'n Flashdragon's tiger 'ad been in the 'abit of driving the Cap'n's vehicle," and that the ragged caitiff he had enlisted as helper, could even help to drive the Influenza!

Poor Joe was now, as formerly the physic basket, covered with oil-skin; oil-skin hat,—oil-skin cape, oil-skin horse-cloth for old Peg, the influenza mare.—And well for *him* the precaution!—For hours together was it his fortune to sit at the doors of old ladies "long-a-dying," old gentlemen reluctant to go out of the world, or young ones deliberate in coming into it. For two whole years, were he and Peg rained upon,—snowed upon,—hailed upon,— blown upon by winds from East, West, North, and South. He became as inured to storms as a weather-cock on a steeple; and it must be admitted that he looked almost as rusty.

He was now a lanky lad of eighteen,—neither man nor boy. To hold the ribands in a more elevated situation was, he knew, impossible, the very vocation of coachee presupposing the word MAN;—for who ever heard of a coach-boy, or coach-hobblede hoy?—Joe was consequently wise enough to stick, like an adhesive plaster, to the apothecary; albeit despising him from his soul, "as a feller wot knew no more of druving than if so be he'd never 'ad a vhip in his 'and!" Just as a Pombal or a Walpole may look down upon the sovereign he holds in subjection, did Joe Tims despise the inefficiency of the apothecary whom it was *his* business to drive!

A terrible event was the cause of his separating from Influenza Peg. Obadiah Senna, after passing for thirty years as an apothecary of unblemished reputation, a punctual payer of parish rates, an indefatigable vestryman, and active private of the Bloomsbury Volunteers, came, in the fifty-ninth year of his age, to be brought up by Crowner's Quest law, on suspicion of woman-slaughter,— even that of Hester Senna, his wife!

Though sufficiently lucky to satisfy twelve competent jurymen that the late Mrs. Senna had been removed from this vale of tears by "ACCIDENTAL DEATH," most of them, particularly those who were married men, could not help manifesting an opinion, that the accident which had caused tincture of opium to change places on the shelf with the bottle of tincture of rhubarb, from which the old lady was in the habit of administering to herself a daily dose, was a *very* lucky *accident* for the survivor!

The old nurse by whose enmity the nature of Mrs. Senna's last illness had been brought to light, was not the only person who shook her head on the occasion. Evidence was brought before the jury that, in domestic life, Senna was far from being mild as emulsion; and, though honourably acquitted of malice prepense in the act of delinquency, the feelings of the female portion of the population manifested themselves so vehemently at the interment of the victim, that the widower was recommended by the metropolitan police and other old women, to withdraw from the neighbourhood.

New Zealand, or some other colony as nearly approaching to penal as possible, was just then in vogue; and poor Senna, with a cargo of agricultural and surgical implements, the Mechanic's Vade Mecum, and a London Pharmacopoeia,—drugs from Apothecaries' Hall, and seeds from Minet's,—embarked as an emigrant for a *terra incognita*, where government promised a premium to all persons disposed to eat kangaroos, or be eaten by bush-rangers,—as the Act directs.

Right glad would he have been could he have persuaded Joe Tims to accompany him, and drive his buffalo team, in a land where roads were not. But though Senna was forced to admit that "needs must when the devil drives," and to depart from a mother country so careful over its elderly ladies as not to admit of their being compelled to take the long nap by mistake of their husbands,—Joe saw no "needs must," because the apothecary wanted to drive.—He talked immensely about his native country, and preferred remaining in a land of XXX.

Again, therefore, was the poor whip precipitated from his driving-seat; and very soon became convinced that a character to be asked for in New Zealand, was as good, or rather as bad, as no character at all. It was now his ambition to drive a pair. He had outlived his giggish propensities. The remembrance of his chilly nights at the sick man's door, was pain and Senna to him. But he was assured that "driving a gig and driving a chariot vos two;" that in matters of coachmanship it is more than *le premier pas qui coûte*; and that he wanted length, breadth, and thickness, bulk and experience, for a coachman.

Joe Tims was almost in despair. One only resource presented itself; and against that, his spirit rebelled, *i.e.* to become a Jarvey! *He*, poor, innocent young man, was unadvised that his coadjutor of the Woolsack had in *his* adversityhood officiated as reporter to a daily paper. And lo! his spirit waxed proud, and he would not hear of a hackney coach.

To be sure, old Peg was not Peacock; but she was an animal of some merit in her way; and the influenza gig a creditable vehicle, and the harness new and wholesome; and, after having presided in a creditable stable, to spend his life in tickling the lean ribs of two wretched brutes, as spare and miserable as himself, rained upon and snowed upon as if still an apothecary's drudge of all work, was a humiliation scarcely to be borne.

To this complexion, however, did he come at last. Joe Tims, proud as old Coutts of his rise in life, is far from unwilling (after a fourth tumbler of stiff punch) to allude to the days when "he druv' number three hundred and forty-five, as neat a cutch as any on the stand."

His enemies have been heard to advert unhandsomely to the wisp of straw which was then all round his old oil-skin hat; and other items of hackney-coachmanly costume, far from mentionable, more especially to a man clothed at this present speaking in purple plush and fine linen. But this is invidious. The body-coachman has never been heard to deny having kept the stand; and it is, probably, to his experience in driving for several years a pair of quadrupeds, (to call them horses were too courtierly,) whereof one was a stumbler and the other a bolter, that he is indebted for his professional skill.

His fare was now harder than ever,—because dependent on his fares. The stand, too, was almost more than he could stand; and the perpetual badge of servitude to which he was condemned badgered him out of his life. More than once, in a fit of just indignation against Providence, he caused himself to be shaven and shorn, sandpapered and scrubbed into presentability, and, having procured a proxy for the day, like some Parliamentary dandy bent upon making holiday at a ball, attempted to procure himself a more honourable post.

But no one would abide the sight of him!—Meagre,—chap-fallen,—out of fashion,—out of favour,—the outline of a man,—the mere hint of a coachman,—with a waist like an opera-dancer's, and cheeks as lank as a black penitent's,—how could he presume to pretend to the honours of a decent coach-box!

He was told—as modern artists of their pictures, and fashionable novelists of their works—that he was much too slight. And lo! in the bitterness of his soul he returned once more to find safety in numbers, and take his stand among his fellows; much marvelling by what process of stuffing his doublet with straw, it might be possible for a poor Jarvey ever to become a man of substance!—

But promotion cometh neither from the east, nor yet from the west. The purple plush of Joe Tims came to him at last out of number three hundred and forty-five! It was his fortune, late one autumn evening, to translate, from a street-corner in the vicinity of Charing Cross, to one of the dingy lunatic-asylum-looking square brick mansions of Bloomsbury Square, a tall perpendicular female, almost as spare as himself, and, consequently, nowise interesting to his feelings beyond the eighteenpence accruing to him from her transit. In the eyes of Joe Tims she was only "fare-ly fair."

But lo! on proceeding next morning to the brushing of the dusty cushions of his detested vehicle, he found, curiously inserted between them, a small parchment-covered pocket-book, mysterious-looking as that of William of Deloraine.

To whom could it belong? Not to the flashy young gentleman he had conveyed from the cigar divan to his lodgings in Mary-le-bone; for *such* people do not deal in parchment-covered pocket-books. Not to the decrepit man he had transported from the neighbourhood of the loan-office to his door at Brompton; for *such* people do not deal in parchment-covered pocket books. Not to the marine-store-keeping family whom he had conveyed pleasuring at per hour to the Zoological Gardens; even *such* people do not deal in parchment covered pocket-books. No! It was evidently the property of some person in particularly easy circumstances; for it contained a register of sums weekly deposited in the savings' bank, without any per contra of sums withdrawn therefrom.

At length, the insertion of a proper name served as some index to the proprietor. "Mistress Ursula Primrose" was the happy proprietor of the pocket-book, and the vested securities of which it treated. Mrs. Ursula Primrose sounded wonderfully like the perpendicular lady of Bloomsbury Square. At all events, it could be no offence to flog the bolter and stumbler thitherwards, and take her legal opinion upon the subject.

Number three hundred and forty-five reached the door. Joe Tims rang at the bell; and the fat footman who responded to the summons, (and whose glazy eyes flashed like a horn lantern when at first he pretended to resent the intrusion of a hackney coachman coming to call, uncalled for, at a genteel residence,) was startled by the mere mention of the name of Mrs. Ursula Primrose into more than Chesterfieldian courtesy. He drew up—he tried to look sober—he almost bowed as he requested Joe to step in, without so much as a glance at his dirty boots, or a hint about the door-mat.

"He would let Mrs. Primrose know that a gentleman wished to speak with her.—What might be his business?"

"His business was with Mrs. Primrose." The body-footman saw that Jarvey was wide awake. He departed; and, after a pause, Mrs. Primrose made her stately *entrée* into the hall, just as Joe was beginning to feel that the smell of roast-beef in the house foretold a cruelly appetizing two o'clock dinner for the Lower House; and to wonder why the fat footman's eyes should look so hazy, while that succulent meal was still in prospect.

But she was no longer the lady of the flowered shawl, patent silk front, and green ankle-boots of the preceding night. Mrs. Primrose was now as yellow as her name,—slatternly, cross, and unpropitious. A portentous frown contracted her brows as Joe first presented himself to her acquaintance. But the sudden change operated in her physiognomy by his production of the parchment-covered pocket-book, would in other centuries have passed for magic! Reversing the old order of things on this occasion, it was the Gorgon's Head itself that became converted into stone.

After a momentary pause, consequent upon this singular petrifaction, she invited Joe to step into the parlour, in a whisper of more than mellifluous sweetness.

"*Did you say anything to John?*"—was Mrs. Ursula's first mysterious inquiry, after closing the door.

Joe diplomatized. He could give no direct answer; for he knew not "John," and could by no means surmise what it was in his power to have communicated to him.—He looked wise, therefore, and shook his head "dubersomely."

Mrs. Ursula's hand was already in her pocket. She had been on the point, like John Gilpin's wife, of "pulling out half-a-crown." But this ominous gesture of the hackney coachman's, like the touch of Midas, converted what she had in her hand into gold.— She pulled out a sovereign.

"*Am I safe?*" said she, in the same mysterious whisper, fixing a terrified and tempting glance upon Joe, as she inserted the coin into his horny palm,—"*I say, am I safe with you?*"—

"*Safe as the Bank!*" cried Joe, with a hackney-coachman-like wink; whereupon, Mrs. Primrose, seeing significance and menace in the familiarity, staggered to a chair.

"*What*, then, are your demands?" said she, in a faint voice. "Will *nothing* tempt you?"

Still blundering and wondering, Joe Tims observed that "he didn't vont no temptation, not he!"

"I know I am in your power!" faltered the agonised housekeeper. "It is the first time as ever I took a glass of anything stronger than spring-water; and I suppose I shall repent it the longest day I have to live. However, I engage to make it worth your while to keep my counsel.—What do you say to a comfortable situation?—Thirty-five guineas a-year,—two liveries,—no night-work,—liberal housekeeping,—and a month's warning ?"

"Say?"—cried Joe Tims, almost as much startled by the offer as Mrs. Ursula Primrose had been by the sight of the parchment-covered pocket-book,—"vy, I should say the lady vos a reg'lar trump vot procured it for me."

A bargain was soon struck,—a blind bargain on the part of Joe; still unable to conjecture what might be the state-secret in his keeping, which had every appearance of being worth a Jew's eye. Nor was it till long after the wisp of straw all round his hat had been exchanged, like Mrs. Primrose's half-crown, for gold,—and his frieze wrap-rascal for a livery as resplendent as consorts with the lustre of the Bloomsburyan world of fashion, that he fully understood the dilemma of the maiden housekeeper of a prudish widow lady, relict of a K.C.—not only convicted of having been taken up at the door of a gin-palace, but agonised by discovery of the loss of her savings'-bank register, conveying in black and white to the least acute observer, the exact amount of her weekly peculations!

She had fancied herself lost, as well as the pocket-book. She had felt convinced that the terrible record would fall into the hands of the police, and be brought back to her lady, whose address it bore. Visions of arraignment,—of restitution,—had rendered her pillow sleepless! No wonder that she conceived the probity of the hackney man to be beyond all praise, if not beyond all reward.

Joseph Tims—we no longer presume to abbreviate the coachMAN—had now abandoned number three hundred and forty-five, to think for the future only of number one.

Regarding him as master of her fatal secret, Mrs. Primrose had not only procured him the place of her lady, Mrs. Creepmouse, but took care to render it a place of pleasantness and peace. Her control over the household was absolute as the sceptre of the Medes and Persians; and not a slave therein had a right to look the new coachman in the face.

The housekeeper doubled the quality of the ale,

> And lo! two puddings smoked upon the board!

Had she been feeding up Joseph for a Smithfield prize, she could not have had tendecare of his diet.

Now Joseph, like the psalmist, was profane enough to find, a divinity in his digestive organs; and it was only natural that she who tended so pamperingly what was his god, should become his goddess. In the strength of the XXXX perhaps consisted his weakness. But by dint of seeing double, he Jehu-diciously ceased to regard Mrs. Ursula as a single woman too spare to become the rib of a thriving coachman. Whether the parchment-covered pocket book were the Ovid in which he conned his art of love, or whether in the dullness of that dullest of dull households—the Lethe's wharf wherein his weediness lay rotting—he fancied his former fare into a fair,—certain it is that, two years after assuming Mrs. Creepmouse's livery, a clandestine marriage converted Ursula Primrose into Ursula Tims, and the parchment-covered pocket-book into a partnership account.

Such was the origin of the comeliness which was the origin of Joseph's progress into Body-Coachmanship.

A long series of hard feeding and soft sleeping produced such an expansion of the outward man of Joseph Tims, that on the decease of the Bloomsbury widow, bequeathing a fat legacy to Mr. and Mrs. Tims, (whose merits and fidelity were set forth in five-and-twenty shillings' worth of legal parchment and engrossing,) the legatee was nearly as fat as his legacy.

From that period, he adhered to his box as a mere matter of pride. He did not choose, not he, though independent, to fling down the reins, and retire into the humdrum obscurity of private life. He could not abide the idea of levees and drawing rooms, at which his ponderous person added no weight to the dignities of the court. He accepted office accordingly in Grosvenor Square; having a second coachman and two scrubs under him, to endure the odium of the screwishness of his government contracts, and grease the wheels of his Jehudicial vocation.

Such is the well-wigged man in authority, to whom, amid the smash of panels, his brother whips of May Fair refer for arbitration. Mr. Tims is a great man,—a householder,—a sound Tory in all but the Corn question. It has been maliciously asserted that, like Lablache when giving tongue in the Puritani, he has an eye to the Royal Box. But we have his own authority to state, that so long as the lovely proprietress of the best-turned-out equipage in town remains contented, her ladyship may reckon upon his faithful service as her BODY-COACHMAN.

The Banker

THERE ARE TWO LEADING CLASSES of London Bankers—the square-toed and the pointed. Of the multifarious qualifications of these human appendages to the moneyed and unmoneyed world, the adnoun most advantageously applicable is the same as to a lady's horse. To be a "safe" man is to be a good banker.

As regards this important distinction, however, neither square-toedness nor pointed-toedness is to be relied on. Of the many unstable firms, which, by anomaly of speech, have figured in the course of the last ten years, in the Gazette, some have been as remarkable for the quizzical and old-fashioned sobriety of the heads of the house, as others for their flashy elegance; the steadiness of the former, and volatility of the latter, being equally a matter of assumption, with a view to increase the cliency of the establishment.

Your sober city-banker is a man who affects, in his shop and his exterior, to possess that within which passeth show. His clothes and manners are homely, his equipage plain, his town and country-houses neat, not gaudy; abounding in solid comfort, but eschewing all pretence to luxurious prodigality.

Josiah Grubbinson chooses it to be perceived by the care he takes of his own money, what care he is capable of taking of the moneys of other people. Sparing and thought-worn, there is nothing in his gravity of brow to encourage indiscreet encroachment on the part of his constituents. The defaulter who knows the *debit* side of his account to be in excess, dare not encounter the repellent aspect of a man who attends divine service thrice on every Sabbath, and has his name inscribed, perforce of ample benefactions, in the hearts of the church-wardens of his parish and the subscription books of all the religious and charitable institutions of the vast metropolis.

So conscientious an individual is not a man to be lightly molested with avowals of need, or the indiscretion that engenders need. He is fenced round by the quickset hedge of his own virtues; intangible as the wooden effigy of a saint in its crystal shrine. Grave, earnest, undemonstrative, it appears almost a crime to hazard the ruffling of so serene a nature. The attempt were as wanton as when perverse children fling stones into a glassy pool, to mar with convolving circles its sacred evenness of surface.

So long as the reserved banker appears quiet

> as a nun,
> Breathless with adoration,

we almost forget that his adoration is simply that of the molten calf,—the most mundane of all idolatries.

The serenity of the banking Tartuffe, meanwhile, is a gift worth twenty per cent. to the firm. "Like loves like!" quoth the vulgate of "*qui se ressemble s'assemble*;" and to the compter of the sober banker, comes the sober citizen; the moderate man, whose moderate gains are sure, and who looks out for a sure banker in whose till to deposit them. Thither rolls the dark and unemblazoned chariot, rumbling from Edmonton after its pair of fat and bean-fed horses, to cash its weekly cheque for its weekly house-accounts. Thither comes the snobby gig, conveying red-faced individuals, whose upper man is thatched with straw, and whose nether man is subjected to the stripes of corduroys. Nay, thither, on Saturdays at even, rattle the market-carts which lack courage to return to Ealing or Battersea Rise with a charge of gold in their weazel skin-purses. The tapsters, who delight in the sobriety of all human beings but their customers, swear that he is the man for their money.

And so he is, by virtually making it his own! So painstaking is the air of the decorous banker, that these happy dupes entertain a vague conviction that he carries about with him in his pockets the exact amount of their balance, not caring to entrust it even to his iron safe!

Nor *does* he. He knows better. The square-toed banker shows how fully he appreciates the value of a deposit by instantly endeavouring to double the amount. Where the stock is so good, it ought to be blessed with increase; procreation of gold being the end and aim of bankermony. The net produce deposited with him by the corduroys and market-carts, accordingly returns unsuspected to their neighbourhood in the suburbs; enkindling the kilns of brick-fields, the furnaces of gas-works; fermenting the vats of breweries, and the stills of distillers. It gallops in mail-coaches; it whirrs along the rail; it crosses the Isthmus of Suez; and disturbs with the paddles of steamboats the tranquil waters of the Niger or Nile, and fœtid canals of China and Batavia.

While the greasy butterman enjoys his quiet afternoon's nap in his parlour at Kennington, or his pew in Ebenezer Chapel, satisfied that his unctuous bank-notes are rotting themselves at ease in a safe in Lombard Street, little does he opine, good easy man! that they are evaporating *in fumo* from forth the tall chimneys of twenty horse-power engines, sinking shafts into the bowels of the earth, or encumbering the surface thereof with the squares and crescents of some new-born watering-place, rising, like Venus of old, from the froth of the sea!

What matters?—His ignorance is bliss.—His money, that is, the money of some newer dupe, is forthcoming at his demand! When he saith, "the funds are low, buy stock," stock is bought, as the stockbroker's receipt avouches; and he lives and dies the happier for having his imprisoned soul taken and lapt in Elysium by his solemn banker; unless, indeed, the gas-works should explode, or the bricks fall—*like* bricks,—carrying with them the unstable firm and its square-toed commander-in-chief.

Even then, he scarcely finds it in his conscience to complain. He is reminded by a circular, as plausible as the face of his grave deceiver, "how strenuously Mr. Josiah Grubbinson laboured against the adverse nature of the times, devoting himself with all his soul, and with all his strength, to business, for the sole profit and advantage of, his constituents; how his head grew white, and his cheeks wrinkled, for very zeal in their behalf: and how, when he found that the pressure of the crisis rendered it impossible for the house to go on, he instantly closed it."

Such is the usual drift of similar addresses. If he inquire, on the other hand, with insolent pertinacity, for the title-deeds of the family estate in Kent, he will be referred to the marriage settlement of Mrs. Josiah Grubbinson. The house in Bedford Square is the property of the eldest son; the villa at Wandsworth was bequeathed by an aunt to the younger children. Mr. Josiah Grubbinson's "robe, and his integrity to Heaven" are all he has to surrender in Basinghall Street!

Nevertheless, the fellow in corduroys is required to compassionate the wealthy banker, who, "after going through life so respectably," is reduced to ruin! He is told he must be a brute not to feel for the mortification of one whose honest name is hoisted into the Gazette, after having figured in deputations to the Chancellor of the Exchequer, in finance-committees, in royal and imperial loans, and, above all, in lists of subscriptions to county hospitals, lunatic asylums, and refuges for the destitute.

How can he refuse, under such circumstances, to sign the certificate of a worthy individual, so oppressed by the evil juncture of the times, ruined by the war in Affghanistan, and overturned by an Oregon panic? Besides, Mr. Josiah Grubbinson has no idea of resuming business as a banker. It is his intention to retire into private life, in his wife's country-seat in Kent, his son's mansion in Bedford Square, and his daughter's villa at East Wandsworth. The fatigues of the speculations undertaken for the benefit of his cliency, have impaired his constitution, and made him old before his time. His day for work is over. All he asks is to live. *Otium—otium* without *dignitate*, is the utmost to which he aspires. Those who wish to speculate in gas-works and brickfields, may go and speculate for themselves.

Reverse wrong is not always right, nor reverse of right always wrong. But the very reverse of the solemn or square-toed banker is he of the West End, Sir Eustatius Consols, who spins his cobwebs of golden wire in the sunshine of life, instead of the shade; and who, instead of delivering his guineas in a copper-shovel to his customer, serves out his half-pence in one of precious metal. This Chesterfield of money-dealers belongs to the vast family of the Surfaces. Everything about himself, or his establishment, is varnished and burnished.

Dress, equipage, house, furniture, fruit, flowers, society,—everything is *optissime*, everything forced. Having begun life with an aristocratic alliance, by marrying the fiftieth cousin of a needy Scotch or Irish Lord, he pursues his system by sending his sons to Eton, and his daughters to Madame Michau's, all for the good of the firm. For the good of the firm, he grows prize peaches, and feeds prize merinos, duly advertised by the Morning Post. For the good of the firm, he gives weekly dinner-parties, and monthly balls or concerts throughout the season. For the good of the firm, his wife's diamonds are reset at Mortimer and Hunt's, to glitter at the drawing room. For the good of the firm, his new carriage is seen, brilliant but substantial, in front of Houlditch's shop.

Quick-sighted, and far-sighted, he has as ready an eye to the shop as John Gilpin of old. At some public *fête*, he picks up the fan of a duchess; and, instead of instantly returning it, like a simply civil man, carries it off in his pocket, to send it back the following morning with a flummering note, calculated to impress indelibly upon the mind of her Grace the name of the Sir Eustatius Consols who presents compliments in so smart a running hand.

You see him shaking hands with some flashy but penniless younger brother, or fetching a chair for some girl of moderate fortune, and wonder why. *Why*, indeed! but that because from his box at the opera the canny banker has watched a showy Honourable Close at the ear of Eve; calling blushes to the cheeks of the fair widow of one of the unfairest—*Anglicè*, richest—of nabobs; and has been the first to discover that the pretty girl has bagged the heir-apparent of the wealthiest dukedom in the three kingdoms.

Certain fools have been obtuse enough to cavil at Lady Consol's box at the Opera as un-bankerish and prodigal. Bless their five wits! It plays its part to admiration, for the good of the firm.

Examine her ladyship's visiting-list, or rather, the lists of invitations to her entertainments (for she is a great deal too far north to invite her poor relations of twenty descents, to her house,) and you will find that all is according to Cocker. Not a name but might stand for a cipher. Not an individual but is translateable into realty or personalty. "Sir Hogmore and Lady Pigwiggin, ten thousand a year in the Fens." "Mr. and Mrs. Groylyn Rugmouth, mines to the tune of hundreds of thousands." "Lord and Lady Frowsyfusty, worth their weight (and what a weight!) in gold!"

Examine the light of their respective countenances, Sir Eustatius at the door of the supper-room,—Lady Consols, of the ball-room,—pressing their civilities on their customers, past, present, or to come. What urbanity, what courtliness, what flexibility of vertebræ and knees. The courtesy of Lady Consols to a dowager duchess with a sufficient jointure, is a thing of caoutchouc; and when she shines forth upon some heiress who has bought her way out of Aldermanbury into the baronetage, it is like the expansion of a July sun at noonday!

People love to be toadied. The rich crowd to the well-lighted, well-refreshmented *fêtes* of Sir Eustatius Consols, season after season, year after year, till, insensibly, intimacy is begotten. On the failure or retirement of their banker, they recall to mind the persevering civilities of these hospitable hosts.

"After all, they cannot choose a safer man than Sir Eustatius!—Sir Eustatius is one so completely above the world.—So much evidence of comfort and abundance in his establishment!—Nothing wanting!—Old wines, young horses, new pictures, old masters, new carriages, old servants. It has become almost a bounden duty with them to bank with Sir Eustatius!"

Sir Eustatius and Lady Consols are, in fact, a sort of Monsieur and Madame Nontongpaw of fashionable life. You ask in the park, "To whom belongs that fine pair of bays?"—"To Lady Consols." You inquire at Madame Devy's for whom they are making that magnificent court-dress, trimmed with point?—"For Lady Consols." You admire at Kitching's a set of emeralds.—"They are for Lady Consols." You wish to secure Jullien's band for your ball.—"He is engaged to Lady Consols." You think of giving a concert. Not one of the Italian singers but has taken earnest from Lady Consols!—But neither the bays, the point, the emeralds, the French orchestra, nor Italian chorus, are appreciated by her ladyship for their sake, or her own. It is simply essential to her to make her house and person agreeable to those she is desirous to conciliate, as hosts or guests, in order that Sir Eustatius may conciliate them as customers. Her cast of the net is a bold one; her angling is angling with a golden hook; and unless the draught, or take, of fishes, be little short of miraculous, the game can scarcely pay. To deal with the great world, it is essential that out of every three persons, two should be able to defray the cost of the third; and, for every Duke with a splendid rent-roll, there are poor relations, spunging friends, and swindling dependants to be compromised withal, who not unfrequently render them a profitless bargain.

A house of business of this description necessarily comprehends a baronet, and a member of parliament. The "Bart." looks well in the printed cheques; while the senatorial dignity extends the connexion of the house, and brings it into hook and crook with the Chancellor of the Exchequer. In former days, franking went for something, by saving a couple of hundreds per annum to the firm. But, even under the domination of penny postage, election expenses repay themselves by the divinity that doth hedge an M.P. in the eyes of smaller constituents; and the consequence of a vote to be conciliated, in those of the greater. A seat in parliament is, consequently, a species of underwriting to a banker.

If one wished to adduce a modern example of the Dives in purple and fine linen of modern times, it should be in the form of a thriving London banker. Their lives exhibit the comfortable in quintessential comfort. A Duke, with a rent-roll of one hundred thousand pounds per annum, is often at a loss for a fifty-pound note—nay, for less. A Duke is preyed upon by auditors, agents, stewards, bailiffs, attorneys, bankers. But the banker is king over his own till. Money is power; and over money, *his* power is great. His foot is upon the necks of the proud, and over the fiercest of the aristocracy doth he cast his shoe. But the shoe thus cast must be of such costly materials, that it is more than problematical whether a Crœsus of the counter, of this description, is to be considered a safe man!

It is amusing to observe what strange specifications enhance the prosperity of certain bankers. By force of affinity, one man succeeds with the Dissenters, another with the Quakers, a third with the Evangelical, a fourth with the theatrical world—(and a hit or miss order of success it is!)—The connection of one firm lies with the agricultural interest, of another with America, of a third with Cochinchina. The jargon and legerdemain of the whole tribe is, however, much the same.

> Welcome ever smiles,
>   And Farewell goes out sighing;

a low bow for a large deposit,—a blank stare at a large demand.

In these days of literary destitution, a private secretaryship to a London banker might not be so bad a place to apply for; the reader to a theatre or a publisher not having half so great a call upon his discretion or powers of language, as such a functionary.

Every moneyed man, or rather every man having the reputation of a capitalist, and the misfortune of having banked with an insecure firm, must have had occasion to admire, on the failure of his banker, the number and eloquence of the missives addressed to him in solicitation of his custom. He finds himself suddenly hoisted upon a pedestal, with a dozen servile money-spinners crawling in the dust at his feet. But after having made his election, he is not a little diverted to perceive the change of tone in the very first letter addressed to him by the new chancellor of his empty exchequer. The superlatives have already subsided into comparatives. Mr. Grubbinson, who was his most obedient humble servant in 1841, becomes his obedient humble servant in 1842, and his obedient servant in 1843. On the first overdrawing of his account, he is addressed by Grubbinson as Grubbinson and Co.; and, in case of a lagging remittance or dishonoured bill, is informed by him, "for partners and self," that it has been "the uniform practice of the house," or "the immemorial custom of their management of business," &c. &c. &c. After having dragged you by the ears into their books, they use just as little ceremony in kicking you out of them.

But to manage the intermedial negociations, the coaxing in and bowing out of Grubbinson's shop, perforce of correspondence, requires no trifling exercise of secretarial prudence. When personally effected, the tact of Grubbinson by himself Grubbinson, alone suffices. The man hardens or softens towards the fluctuating constituent, like a bar of iron in a forge. There is as wide a difference between the countenance that says "Good day!" to the man of thousands and that which, the following minute, says, "Get along about your business!" to one in arrear of hundreds,—as between the winter and summer solstice!

Safer than either the rigidly severe or irregularly obliging banker, is the one between Squaretoes and Pointed, who neither solicits business nor rejects it; satisfied with the cliency bequeathed to him by his predecessor, and sure to surrender it undiminished by ungraciousness, as unendangered by irregular concessions, to those who shall succeed him; pursuing the even tenour of his social way, without regard to the conciliation of business and creating no intertanglement between his counter and his dining-table.

The business of private banking is supposed to have been greatly diminished of late years by the increase of commercial or joint-stock banks. We doubt whether the preference thus accorded be half so much conceded to prejudice or faith in the greater security in these public concerns, as to the absence of offence in the person of the banker.

The manager or superintendent of these concerns is a species of irresponsible and disinterested intermediary, who has no object in picking your pocket, or throwing dust, even if gold dust, into your eyes. You run no risk of being affronted through his means by an invitation to tea, when you feel that your account intitles you to be asked to dinner. He is an influence rather than an individual. You would as soon think of feeling piqued at his deportment as by some dispensation of Providence. It matters not to you whether he drive a barouche or gig, or even adventure the infamy of a hack-cab. He has his stipend, as nominated in the bond, nor more nor less; and to play at ducks and drakes with your money, in the rashness of speculation, would not advance him a doit. He advertises not his dinners in the Morning Post, nor does his wife give balls or concerts;—the better chance that his name will never figure in an uttermost corner of some Wednesday's or Monday's morning paper, in a citation from that exterminating document, the London Gazette!—

Be it noticed, among the notabilia of the moneyed world, that there are in London one or more banking houses, whose books of business extend back from the reign of Victoria to that of Elizabeth, where, under the name of goldsmiths, curious items of credit appear therein, such as goblets, tankards, and apostle spoons. These books constitute invaluable historical archives, besides conveying a patent of commercial nobility; when, as in certain instances we could point out, the banker of to-day descends in direct line, and inherits the identical patronymic of the goldsmith his ancestor,—even as

> An Amurath an Amurath succeed,
> And Harry, Harry.

This is the very legitimacy and conservatism of the kingdom of Mammon. This is an indisputable attestation of hereditary prudence and probity. Such a standing in commercial life becomes a sort of second conscience. Three centuries of trustworthiness!— twelve reigns of financial discretion! It amounts, in business-life, to a barony connected with Magna Charta in the aristocratic!

Most of the prominent financial demigods, however, are men of yesterday,—individuals whom Fortune has rolled to the top of her wheel by a single turn, perhaps to be rolled back again with similar precipitation. The greatest Jewish names in the moneyed world are names unknown to the eighteenth century, and which the nineteenth may be reserving to

> Point a moral and adorn a tale.

Even Rothschild commenced his prosperity at Frankfort at the coronation of the late Emperor of Austria, by selling copper medals commemorative of the event, (in company with his sister,) at a beer house of the city.

The life, influence, and connections of Coutts will one day become historical, conveying a great moral lesson as regards the frailties and follies at which the worshippers of Mammon, even of the highest grade and repute, will connive, in pursuance of their vile idolatry;—how they will swallow the camels forced upon them by a rich banker, and strain at the gnats buzzing round the head of uninfluential penury.

The thriving London banker of the Coutts order is, in fact, a Sir Oracle. Your Privy Councillor sings small to him;—your learned magistrate defers to his decree;—the thews and sinews of the war of life lie at his disposal. At his nod, the sluice-gates close or open which control the fate of a country, and the destinies of thousands. The Sultan is not more absolute. When he concedes, the world applauds his liberality,—where he withholds, his prudence. His penuriousness is foresight,—his weakness magnanimity. Whether close-fisted or open, a great banker can do no wrong—*i.e.* till his docket is struck.

More would we say; but be a simple anecdote the apology for our discretion. Some one was complaining to a popular lawyer of the inconvenience he had sustained from the failure of his banker. "You should do as I do," replied the cautious friend. "*I* am never inconvenienced. I have *two* bankers;—and overdraw both."

On this hint, having become the banker of our own banker, the less we say the better in elucidation of the mysteries of the calling. Nay, truth to tell, howbeit we have no house of business in Lombard Street, we entertain a wondrous degree of fellow-feeling towards—the London Banker.

The Hotel-Keeper

"MINE HOST," WHETHER OF THE Garter or Star, was formerly a mighty pleasant fellow—drank and jested with his customers, making them pay for his jokes and potations. In the present day, when the diffusion of classes render their fusion more difficult, (so that human beings are stuck up in rows in the world, like plants in the horticultural gardens, classed and labelled, stiff as the sticks that intercept them,) you pay for the wine and pastime of your host, but without participating in the entertainment.

Mine host of the Hotel, is a well-bred gentleman, whom its inmates never behold from the day when he inaugurates them in their apartments, with as many bows as would place an unpopular candidate at the head of the poll, to that on which, with similar ceremonial, he presents them their bill;—as though a highwayman were to make three glissades and a coupé, preparatory to his "Your money or your life!" The Hotel-keeper is usually some noble man's maître d'hôtel, or groom of the chambers, made an honest man of in holy matrimony by her ladyship's confidential maid or consequential housekeeper; who invests their united earnings, perquisites, pickings, (and no matter for the *last* word of the indictment,) in furnishing and burnishing some roomy mansion of the West-end, too much out of repair to serve as a private residence, for "noblemen and gentlemen," by dint of showy calico, stained mahogany, and half the brass of a whole Birmingham foundry; thereby intitling themselves to demand, as the rent of every separate suite of apartments, as much as the whole house would have cost, if hired for the season.

Prodigious four-post beds, groaning with draperies and fringes, destined to accumulate dust, soot, and their living concomitants, for ten years to come, are erected in the sleeping rooms, with as much labour and ingenuity as are employed to run up a three-storied house in the suburbs;—with rickety wardrobes and washing-stands, picked up at sales, or purchased at cheap and nasty furniture-brokers in the Blackfriars Road,—whereof it is hazardous to open a drawer, not only on account of the effluvium of the boots or shoes of antecedent occupants, but from the certainty that three-quarters of an hour must be wasted in shoving, sidling, and swerving the said ill fitting drawer back into its original position.

For the same reason, the prudent frequenter of a London hotel is careful not to draw down a blind, of the impossibility of ever getting it up again;—or to undraw a curtain, from the clouds of dust instantly circulating through the apartment. The blind so displaced, or the drawer thus incautiously drawn forth, is moreover sure to be recalled to his memory by a charge in the bill for repairing the same; such as

	s.	d.
To man one day repairing Blind	17	6
Cords, &c., for do.	6	10
Easing Drawer, strained	10	6
&c. &c.	&c.	

To touch the handle of a China or marble vase, is equally rash. Pooloo's cement will not last for ever; and when you find the vase standing handle-less before you, like a door from which some slang-loving roué has wrenched off the knocker, but with evident symptoms of the glue of preceding fractures and mending, be assured that you will have to book up the full original cost of the "handsome vase of Nankin dragon China, finely enamelled," which was purchased damaged at a sale ten years before, and has been successively paid for by twenty victims, inhabitants of the same unlucky suite.

The first object of the hotel-keeper, after fitting up his rooms with gaudy papers, showy carpets, and trophies and cornices of gilt brass, is to purchase vast services of iron-stone China, and plated dishes and covers, which, on an emergency, when the families under his roof are sufficiently frantic or unfortunate to dine at home, he fills with parsley beds; in the centre of which, by dint of much examination and a powerful glass, are discoverable a thin slice of cod or salmon, or a couple of fried whitings—a few chips of cutlets—a starveling cat roasted rabbitwise, or a brace of sparrows deluged in parsley and butter, designated in the bill of fare as pigeons or chickens.

The second course will probably be a bread pudding, formed of the crumbs that fall from the rich man's table; or a tart, apparently composed of buff leather and mouldy fruit, having been allowed to mellow for a week in the larder, in company with the Stilton cheese. But then, it is served on a lordly dish, and covered with an embossed cover.

Such is the moderate *mem.* of an hotel dinner. Its gaudy days are still harder of digestion; the worst viands, charged at the highest rate; meagre poultry—stale vegetables—doubtful fish. It is not the host who has to eat them; and the fashion of the olden time, of allotting him his share of the repast, was surely so far advantageous, that it operated like the functions of the carver and taster at a royal banquet, as a security against being poisoned in cold blood.

On the same grounds, in choosing an hotel, it is always desirable to select one to which, like the Clarendon, a coffee-room is attached. Those which are not furnished with such a gastronomic safety-valve, are compelled (though not by Act of Parliament) to consume their own scraps; devouring in patties or a currie on Monday, the lobster they pronounced impossible on the Saturday preceding; and swallowing in the shape of oyster sauce, the repellent reptiles abhorently left on their plates at supper over night.

It is horrific to think of the number of times the same articles of food are made to figure at the table,

Wearing strange shapes, and bearing many names.

In certain cases, where the Hotel-keeper has risen to his dignity as a householder from the post of head-waiter at a coffee-house, the evil is increased by his bringing in the first dish, and doing the honours of his soup,—a square of portable, dissolved in tepid water, and tasting sorely of the copper of a plated soup-tureen, the metallic poison being counteracted by a handful of coarse spices, and sufficient pepper to devil a whole poultry-yard. But the gentleman host is so well got up, and his specious laudation of the excellence of his cook is so pompously delivered, that you prefer choaking in silence to disputing the point. By *his* account (both verbally and clerkly delivered), you have turtle and venison before you, if you had only sense or appetite to find it out; and in spite of the evidence that it is mere roast and boiled, (the roast being a chip of the old block, and the water which the lamb or chicken was seethed in having been already brought you to wash your hands), you wisely prefer acquiescence, in order to dismiss to his evening paper and sloe-juice negus, the individual who stands wheezing over you, with an eye to his bill, and an ear to what gossip he can pick up from your table-talk.

On the Continent, hotel-keepers are uniformly in the pay of the police. In London, they exercise an inquisition of their own, of which their waiters are the familiars. Not a note or letter passing through the hands of these worthies but assumes a rotundiform shape, from the bulging to which it has been subjected ;—and every night, when the head-waiter carries in his daily evidence to the book-keeper of the wine, soda-water, and other extras consumed by the inmates, he accompanies his account with particulars of visits and visitors, letters, and duns, which, by dint of prying into drawers and loitering on stair cases, he has been able to amass, mismatch, and weave into a tissue of scandal.

He "has his suspicions that the gentleman in black whom Sir Thomas calls his solicitor, and to whom he is never to be denied, is no better than a money-lender; and as to the handsome Colonel, who calls every day at five, being a cousin of the gay widow on the second floor—he knows better!"

An important branch of consumption in hotels consists in the potables. During his aristocratic service, the hotel-keeper, when waiting at table as maître d'hôtel, being accustomed to hear frequent remarks that nothing was more injurious to wine than the rumbling of carts and carriages over the cellars, he provides against such an injury by laying in no stock to be rumbled over; but contents himself with having in his fresh-brewed port or sherry from an advertising shop in the Strand,—per cart, weekly,—or per barrow, daily. It is only his soda-water, which, being uninjurable by street rumbling, he keeps by him from year to year. To ask for French wines in the common run of London hotels, is an act of intrepidity only excusable in such as are scientifically curious in chemical compounds.

It is scarcely possible for the least inquisitorial frequenter of an hotel to remain unconscious or insensible to his fellow lodgers. Thanks to the thinness of partitions and a common staircase, he becomes painfully and reluctantly participant in their family secrets. A sympathy is inevitably begotten. He not only dines upon their fillet of veal, minced, or sends his fillet to them minced in his turn,—he not only resigns himself to their potatoes washed, or inflicts upon them his drumsticks of a chicken in a fricassée,—but is unpleasantly apprised by oral evidence when the ears of her ladyship's daughters have been boxed, or when her ladyship's self has been subjected to conjugal objurgation for the price of her box at the Opera.

He is kept awake till daybreak, morning after morning, by two charming sisters prattling their mutual confidences in an adjoining room, while curling their hair after their balls, or by the sobbings of the lady's-maid after a universal blowing-up. By the scent of the towels placed on his stand, screwed into a dry linen press, instead of being subjected to the washing-tub between service and service, he is able to ascertain whether his fair neighbours prefer eau-de-cologne to lavender-water, or indulge in Barèges baths; and without exercising the baleful scrutiny of the head-waiter, is compelled to know *when* they are waiting for the milliner, or when they are "at home only to the Captain."

The Hotel-keeper, meanwhile snugly ensconced in his private room, like the spider which, retired into a corner of its web, watches the simple flies gradually entangling themselves in its meshes, takes care only that the brills which figure on the table shall figure in the ledger as turbots with lobster-sauce, and that the heads of the woodcocks and pheasants shall be kept sacred as that of the Baptist, in order to consecrate dishes of hashed mutton, to appear hereafter as *salmis de bécasse* or *de faisan* ;—writing down teas for tea,—coffees for coffee ; and every Sunday afternoon, converting in the standing accounts the every 5s. 0d. into 5s. 6d., and every 2s. 0d. into 2s. 9d., by the addition of a curly tail above or below zero.

Another important branch of his business is to take care that the dinners be not *too* appetizing; that the bread be stale enough,—the Stilton new enough,—the lamb old,—the mutton young,—the beef coarse as if from the bulls of Basan;—the coffee weak,—the viands strong!

Aware that a family having taken root in his house, and, by sending forth their visiting cards, declared it their domicile for the season, is not likely to be at the trouble of striking its tents and removing else where, his zeal abates from week to week of their sojourn. The only individual to whom he is at the trouble of making his house agreeable is some wealthy minor, who pays interest per annum for a bill, to be discharged when he attains his majority; or foreigners of distinction, by whose courier he is kept in awe, because at some future season the gentleman in gold lace and jack-boots may have the bear-leading of other princes from Krim Tartary, or dukes from the Two Sicilies.

With all their penalties on purse and comfort, however, the London Hotels afford a satisfactory relief from the cares of temporary housekeeping. Deaths, marriages, or baptisms, in country families, involving brief and sudden visits to the metropolis, would otherwise be scarcely carried on with decency The happy wretch relieved from an East India voyage,—the *un*happy one subpœnaed for a Chancery suit,—sees in the gas-lamps blazing over the door of a fashionable hotel, a beacon of hope. The courteous welcome of the cringing host and bowing waiters, appears auspicious. Everything comes with a call. In one's own domicile, a ring of the bell is an injury inflicted on one or more members of the establishment, who have nothing to gain by answering the summons. But in an hotel, every ring secures expenditure, varying from twelve-pence to a guinea. Coals, a sandwich, nay, even a candle to seal a letter, becomes an item to swell the amount of the narrow folios arrayed against the peace and purse of the lodger. Satisfy your conscience, therefore, oh ye who sojourn in hotels, that, give as much trouble as ye may, none but yourselves are the worse for it. A hotel-keeper knows how to value a perpetual ringer of bells!

Among the memorabilia of hotels is the ubiquity and insomnolency of head-waiters. At all hours of the day and night, these wretched creatures are primed for service. The family which returns at four from a ball, or the family which rises at five to start on a journey, finds them equally alert; after having at all the tables, and slaved after all the rings of all the bells the preceding day. It may be doubted, indeed, whether they behold their beds throughout the season,—a slight ablution or change of wig, being their utmost refreshment. Hence the curious weazened old-boyish air of this peculiar and much enduring race of men; compelled to bow submission to as many masters as the toad lying under the harrow, when "Ilka tooth gives her a tug!"

Let nothing aforesaid be supposed to impugn the venerable dignity of the Clarendon, or the comfort and refinement of Mivart's *appartement des Princes*. These, and many others, are as excellent as their high reputation. Moreover, if people choose to be victimized by less conscientious hotel-keepers, the act is their own. When an Irish peer adduced to an hotel-keeper a charge of three-and-sixpence a bottle for soda-water in a former bill, as a reason for having betaken himself elsewhere, mine host urbanely replied, "Your lordship ought to have told me what you intended to give. When properly arranged with, I charge as reasonably as anybody."—What can an hotel-keeper say more?

But for this highway and byway robbery during the harvest of the season, how, in fact, could the hotel-keeper enable himself to get through the autumn, when his house might just as well be closed as Her Majesty's theatre, for any moneys taken at the doors.

Saving painters and whitewashers, not a soul crosses his threshold, unless now and then some skinflint of a dowager on her way through London from Broadstairs, to her dower-house in some midland county; who, saving for the sops of her parrot and board of her maid, expends not a sixpence in the hotel;—or a brace of tender parents conveying some young hopeful to Eton, and spending four-and-twenty reluctant hours in London, for a preparatory visit to the dentist.

For six or eight months, in short, every caravanserai stands empty as the heads of the honourables and lordlings who frequent it in May and July; its kitchen-range rusting; its curtains and hangings being required to "down with their dust," instead of its customers. Nevertheless, rent, taxes, and waiters, must be paid as regularly as if the hotel-keeper were not taking his pleasure at Ramsgate, and his customers at three hundred miles distance. And how is this to be effected, we should like to know, unless by charging three-and-sixpence a bottle for soda water, while the sun shines, and the town is crowded?

But if there be something unspeakably dolorous and funereal in the autumnal aspect of a fashionable hotel, there are few things pleasanter than its countenance in June. When the summer days are at their longest, the hall is thronged with liveries of every dye; and a perpetual discharge of milliners' baskets and jewellers' cases encumbers the lobby.

The landed gentry who arrive in town from their country seats, come for the express purpose of spending and enjoying. The business of their visit to the metropolis, is pleasure. They come to present their daughters, attend levees and drawing-rooms, get invited to the Court balls, if they can; and if not, content themselves with Almack's and the Caledonian.

Such people take wondrous delight in a new bonnet, are much addicted to fine feathers and French ribbons; frequenting the Zoological Gardens on Sundays, and the Horticultural for every fête. Not over-choice in their diversions, they amuse themselves without intermission. Operas, plays, balls, parties, dinners, *déjeûners*, exhibitions, fill up the round of every merry, busy, bustling day. Carriages stand at the doors of the hotels, at an hour when the doorways of private mansions are fast asleep. There are pretty sure to be children in the house, to insure Punch or the Fantoccini stopping before it; and not an itinerant band but strikes up its Strauss and Labitsky under the windows of the London Hotel. There, caper the dancing dogs—there, stalk the conjurors on stilts—there, tumble the tumblers! Small change is never wanting at the receipt of custom; and of these itinerant showmen, some secure retaining from the nursery, others gratuity of dismissal from the drawing-room.

Throughout the morning, one mountebank succeeds to another; and the moment the lamps are lighted for dinner, the *cornet-à-piston* and his fellow conspirators against public comfort, commence their clang; while, clustered before the door, stand family-coaches, chariots, and well-appointed cabs, waiting to convey the country-cousin, to the Opera, or French play. Oh! joyous merry-go-round life of pleasure!—Oh! laborious toil and labour of the do-nothings!—where are you more actively, or more brilliantly carried on, than in the neighbourhood of the fashionable hotels

Next in importance to the London Hotel, are those of the watering places. Brighton and Cheltenham, Harrogate and Tunbridge Wells, vie, indeed, with the hostelries of the metropolis, or perhaps excel them, their season being more definite and incisive. As regards pantry and buttery hatch, they are better provided; and for the reason which enhances the merits of the Clarendon—the appendix of a coffee-room or ordinary. At the minor bathing places the case is different; the apartments being more finely and flimsily furnished than those of London, the table more villanously provided.

The nearest approach, by the way, to the ancient hostel and host of former times, exists, or till the invention of railroads, did exist, in certain crack stages of the old North Road; inns of good dimension and repute, where the mail-coach supped or dined, and the great northern families stopped to sleep ;—where portly sirloins, huge rounds of beef, hams of inviting complexion, fowls, supportable even after those of dainty London, spitch-cocked eels, and compôtes of wine-sours, were evermore forthcoming on demand.

What home-brewed—what home-baked—what cream-cheeses—what snow-white linen—what airy chambers—and what a jolly-faced old gentleman, and comely old gentlewoman, to bid you welcome. It was a pleasure to arrive—a pain to depart. The very Boots seemed to receive his gratuity reluctantly. The waiters *really* wished you a safe and pleasant journey. The chamber maid, after keeping you in hot water during your stay, gave you a warm farewell. There was a barn-yard homeliness of good cheer about the place, how different from the flashy gaudiness of a station-house albergo! One experienced a feeling of cordial good-will towards the broad-faced old gentleman in velveteens and a buff waistcoat who, bowing on his doorstep officiated in such a spot as—the HOTEL-KEEPER.

The Private Secretary

OF PRIVATE SECRETARIES THERE ARE two species; the one, a piece of mechanism in the hands of an expert official; the other, endowed with grace, wisdom, and understanding,—an invisible intelligence, actuating the measures of some nonentity of gentle blood thrust forward in public life upon the pedestal of high connexion.

Among the callings for which a legible hand and decent orthography are supposed to constitute the necessary qualifications, that of the Private Secretary is the most speculative, and least plebeian. The clerk, the usher, are gents or snobs; the Private Secretary is an esquire and a gentleman. In former times, indeed, none but Statesmen or Ambassadors pretended to retain such onerous appendages in their households; and to be even the tag-rag or bob tail of a plenipo' or a cabinet-minister, afforded a fairer opening for "a genteel youth," than to be a clerk in the Treasury, or at Child's.

But now-a-days every rich man who cannot spell, every itinerant actor, every manager of a theatre, has his private secretary; and the vocation has, consequently, forfeited caste. If you send to order the dancing-dogs or galante-show to amuse your nursery, you will receive an answer to your verbal message, indited by Signore Katterfelto's private secretary; while most of the Marchionesses and Countesses, who constitute what is called by the newspapers "the *leaders* of ton," (as though fashionable life were a *drag*!) entertain some hanger on,—some elderly Miss of good education,—who answers their Almack's notes, and enacts the part of honorary secretary.

The province of the first description of Private Secretary to which we have adverted, the mere pen-in-hand of an expert official, is to indite circulars under dictation, or letters marked "private and confidential," though containing no sort of information susceptible of being divulged; answers to petitions or requests, which convey neither negative nor affirmative,—wordy phrases, intended to engender hope, but which when analyzed are found to contain neither pledge nor promise. A well-trained ministerial secretary will string you together plausible sentences, as boys the empty shells of bird's-eggs,—fair and specious-looking things, filled with innutritious air, and signifying nothing!

Generally speaking, your *very* great man selects for his Private Secretary some, honourable nephew or cousin; partly on the grounds of the Antiquary's adage, that "We give our ain fish-guts to our ain sea-mews;" and partly for the better assurance of his zeal and trustworthiness, the two noble kinsmen necessarily hanging together, or hanging separately.

But the *active* public man of business, the minister who is not too fine a gentleman to give audience in the first person singular, who wants no showy substitute to bow out the intrusions of faithful public servants bringing grievances to be redressed, or claims to be examined, usually attaches to himself some intelligent young fellow, with competent knowledge of the law and the world, and spirit to point out a blunder to his employer; as well as the νους to detect it.

To such a man, a private secretaryship is a secure stepping-stone to preferment. Brought into collision with the most eminent men of the day, not alone do his faculties become brightened, but he enjoys rare opportunities for their development and exhibition. If clever by nature, it will be his own fault if he do not pass for fifty times cleverer. By modestly keeping in the back-ground while his principal is perpetrating blunders, and afterwards stepping forward adroitly to his extrication, he appears to confer serious obligations; while his opportunities of lavishing minor favours on less important people are beyond computation, though not beyond reward. As the Lord commended the unjust steward, the Lords of the Treasury are pretty sure to be humbugged into advancing the unjust Private Secretary of a cabinet minister.

Certain it is that these privileged individuals, when *really* of a description to be trusted,—*i.e.* when either honourable cousins or nephews, or approved dirty dogs,—become as rich in unsatisfactory secrets as a confessional or a pawnbroker's books. If the chancellor be the keeper of the King's conscience, *they* hold the tariff of the ministers. Newspaper writers, and getters-up of political memoirs, are fond of talking of "the influence behind the throne," or "back-stairs interposition;" meaning, when the sovereign is a young man, his ladies of the bed-chamber, when a young woman, *her* ladies of the bed-chamber. The Private Secretary constitutes the influence behind the throne, and back stairs prompter, of the premier;—enjoying opportunities of playing upon the feelings of even the most upright and inflexible of ministers; for Cato himself might have been influenced under certain circumstances by his favourite amanuensis.

There are moments of fatigue, exhaustion, indigestion, impatience,—moments when smarting under a royal reprimand, or attenuated by long fasting, or gorged with turtle and lime-punch, when the strongest ministerial mind becomes most unstatesman likely enfeebled. At such times, steals in the Private Secretary, sole spectator and sole auditor of the bedrivelment of his patron; and, like the enemy who intruded into the orchard of the sleeping Hamlet,

> Pours into the porches of his ears
> A lep'rous distilment.

On the morrow, or on restoration to him self, who is wiser for the fact that the minister has been made a fool of?—The deed is done! During his fit of weakness he has imbibed an ineffaceable prejudice or erroneous impression. False opinions have taken root in his mind. He displaces the centurion, of whom the private secretary spake reprobatively over-night; and when the pale petitioner who is to have an audience of him at noon, opens his arduous suit, the unhappy victim finds that his case is prejudged.

On the other hand, if, after an extra glass or two of burgundy, or a royal audience of a conciliatory nature, or the perusal of a leading article in a leading government paper, laudatory, and not over-laudatory of his measures, the minister leaves open the gate of his heart to the advances of his sub, nothing so easy as to seize the occasion for naming names, and recording services of the individuals whom the Private Secretary delighteth to honour. Such golden moments are readily turned to account; and the great man conceives himself to be performing a rigid act of public justices when, in fact, played upon like a flute by the cunning artist who has found out his stops. The deserving, though obscure individual whom he glories in having snatched into the sunshine of preferment, is no other than the stupid school-chum of his Private Secretary

Some patrons, whether ministerial, financial, or mercantile men, are careful to employ the hand of a private secretary only in their most moral and translucent transactions. Others keep them precisely for the management of those equivocal negociations in which they do not choose to commit themselves, or act as principal. If they cannot afford to keep a conscience, they keep in its place a private secretary to relieve them of their scruples. The minister who has an enormous falsehood to perpetrate, is pretty sure to do the deed of darkness, vicariously, by the hands of a secretary; and after the fulfilment of such duties, it is astonishing the increase of consequence assumed by the mender of pens,—as though he prided himself on having officiated as a sheet of blotting paper to the character of his employer.

The office of Private Secretary, by the way, appears to exercise considerable influence over the human nature and constitution. Well do we remember a certain idle schoolfellow of ours, one Tom Grosvenor by name, remarkable at Eton only for his duncehood; a frank-hearted chap, as much in favour with his fellow-idlers as in disrepute among the dons.

Five years afterwards, occasional glimpses of Tom in the crush-room at the Opera, or lounging along Pall-Mall in the dog-days, exhibited him in the character of a junior clerk in the Treasury,—idle as ever, listless as ever, ignorant as ever,—but still the same pleasant give-and-take sort of companion,—a bubble on the London stream, likely to evaporate at any hour or moment, and leave not a trace behind.

At that period of his life, Tom was at any man's service; willing to talk, walk, or dine with all and sundry. Not but that he was discriminating enough to dine oftenest where the viands and company were of a daintier description; and though a lounger in half the houses of the West End, was most assiduous in those having Opera-tickets to give away, or a country seat to insure him a little pheasant-shooting in the autumn. With all, however, he was the same open-hearted, or rather free-spoken rattle; the rashest and most indiscreet of chatterboxes, whom no one trusted with a secret, seeing that he made no secret of his own.

That such an individual could aspire to the character of a secretary, seemed an absolute perversion of the title; and when, on a sudden change of ministry, the government papers announced that Thomas Grosvenor, Esq. had been nominated to the office of Private Secretary by the noble lord at the head of the —— department, we agreed, one and all, who had known him at Eton or since, that it could not be our Tom.

It was not till, on seeking him at his Treasury desk a few weeks afterwards, we found a still, idler fellow than himself warming his nether-man on the hearth-rug which he had been accustomed to monopolize four hours in the day for eight months in the year, that we granted our credence to the singular promotion of our quondam friend.

How had it been achieved? There was nothing "private or confidential" about Tom, nay, not so much as a legible handwriting in him towards the making of a private secretary; and we were finally forced to admit, on the assurance of his former comrades, that Tom Grosvenor must have been promoted into Thomas Grosvenor and the Red Book, in consideration of his skill in being beaten every night at chess by the noble lord at the head of the —— department, during a snowy Christmas, when they were spending the holidays together at Guzzlinton Park.

Eager to shake him congratulation-wise by the hand, we soon afterwards called at his lodgings. But he was no more to be found there, than in his old quarters at the Treasury. On week-days, this was accountable enough. But his ready adoption of the of rushing out of town on Sundays, appeared at least premature.

Even from the Opera, our former place of rendezvous, he had disappeared,—that is, disappeared from the pit into the rear of certain boxes connected with ministerial life; and instead of showing his nose in the crush-room, he was now only seen by glimpses, hurrying down stairs during the last scene of the ballet, the great lady of some great lord, shuddering at the mere possibility of not escaping into her carriage before the circulation of the vulgar throng.

When at length we *did* meet, plain was it to be seen that the transformation of Tom into Thomas was not the only one my old schoolfellow had undergone. Instead of the sprawling grasp of former days, given with the right hand or left, as juxtaposition favoured the uncalculated movement, he now advanced his hand perpendicularly, collected into the form of a fish-slice, so as to render a friendly pressure impossible; nor did his brow unbend or his mouth relax as of old into a spontaneous greeting. On the contrary, his lips appeared as if closed, like a despatch-box, by a spring lock; and his glance was as frozen as the Guzzlinton lake during the time he used to play chess, or rather be played upon at chess, by his new patron.

Still, the metamorphosis might be purely extrinsic. Tom and ourselves had too often heard the chimes together at midnight, to admit of his becoming Thomas for us as readily as for the rest of the world; and nothing would have been easier than to overturn the pedestal of dignity on which he seemed disposed to establish himself.

Compulsory familiarity, however, was not what we wanted. A man may be bullied into civility; but becomes an enemy for life to the individual who forces himself on reluctant acknowledgment as a friend. It was a small sacrifice to accept the degree of intimacy the new Secretary chose to assign, and thus perfect our study and contemplation of his character and motives.

At the close of six months, accordingly, we had come to be familiarly admitted into the private room of the Private Secretary thoroughly behind the scenes, so as to examine at leisure the pulleys and levers by which the machinery was worked. While the vulgar throng, without, was envying the easy and brilliant destinies of Tom, his influential position—his dinners with the political world, and balls with the gay—we had occasion to behold the reverse of the tapestry, by witnessing his toils and labours in a thankless vocation; the affronts he was forced to swallow; the vigils he was obliged to keep; the engagements he was compelled to forego.—Rather would we be a dog and bay the moon, than such a Private Secretary!

It is true that, on the other hand, we saw him assume at certain hours his official con sequence, saying to this man "Do!" and he did it; to the other messenger, "Go!" and he went. We watched him mask his visage with that blank and inexpressive vacuity, which an able diplomatist is careful to assume as a vizard, when in contact with intriguing or inquisitive persons. We heard him deny in terms that sounded like assent; and accept, in phrase that sounded like denial.

We have known him reply to, or rather parry with specious and inconclusive generalities, a letter, the contents of which he pretended to have scrupulously examined, but which we knew, from ocular investigation, lay with an unbroken seal within his desk. We have seen him deprecate with bows and congés the wrath of some great man, to whom it was his patron's pleasure to be invisible; or silence, by the coldness and calmness of his reserve, the vituperation of little men to whom he was deputed to convey an open sentence of exclusion.

It was amazing in how short a period he had acquired all these mysteries of the calling: how spontaneously and familiarly he became acquainted with all the myrmidons of the press; how he carried in his pocket the keys of their consciences, and how thoroughly he understood to which of them to delegate the charge of such and such a question:—to which to apply when it was necessary for the truth to be spoken; to which, when it was judged desirable to throw dust in the staring eyes of the public.

Some editor or other was sure to be either seated authoritatively in the armchair of honour of his cabinet, or skulking on his back-stairs. A portion of these were there to pump the Private Secretary, a portion to be pumped. Some, it was his business to cram with false intelligence while from others, he spared no pains to extract the truth. With one or two, he was courteous even to courtliness; with three or four, coarse almost to brutality.

The whole correspondence of his principal appeared to pass through his hands; though it is likely enough that, while he fancied himself in possession of all his official and even ex-official secrets, the specimens which he showed me in attestation of the confidence reposed in him, were by no means those which his patron held nearest his heart. —Nevertheless, the little gilt and perfumed billets concerning which Tom—I beg his pardon,—Thomas Grosvenor, used to consult me while framing a suitable reply, were such as any other man than a minister might have held dear and accounted sacred.

Such touching little appeals, in French, English, and Italian! Such entreaties for an audience, which the gentle dears were careful not to call a rendezvous! Such injunctions to discretion, such adjurations to despatch! Some asking for a secretaryship of legation for a husband, brother, or lover; some simply for a ten pound note for themselves; some imploring for intercession with the Lord Chamberlain for invitations to the royal balls; some demanding as a right the notice of the Court; above all, not a few offering equivalents, and such curious equivalents!—trafficking for coronets, ribands, mitres, baronetcies, lord and commissions with the coin-current of votes in both their Houses, and the tenderest interests of the heart!

One or two were eloquent in reproaches for former benefits forgot; such as "my lord, who has so zealously supported your administration, to be overlooked when you have had three Garters at your disposal within the last six months!" or, "I must say it reflects little honour on the justice and equity of government when such services as those of my poor dear Sir Peter, who has not missed a division for the last twenty years, are passed over in the creation of a batch of peers, which includes such individuals as Sir Rumbleberry Cram, and Mr. Swellington Swellington, of Swellington!—But of this, your lordship will hear elsewhere!"

More touching still, such little reproaches as "*You*, you for whom I have sacrificed, if not my own self-esteem, at least the good opinion of the world (for you well know all that was inferred from your constant visits to our house at Brighton in the winter of 1818!); *you* to refuse me so trifling a favour as the place of tide-waiter for the son of my butler, that pains-taking, devoted servant, whom you cannot but remember waiting upon you at a period so dangerously important to my domestic happiness!"

That such notes were placed, though marked "private and confidential," in the hands of the Secretary to be answered, did not much surprise me. I was only sorry that similar appeals, with reminders of more recent kindnesses, were not equally at his disposal. There is immense instruction in the "private and confidential" billets-doux correspondence of a cabinet minister! So satisfied is the world of his dispositions for intrigue, that, even in the most trivial matters, he is beset by machinations and cabals. The Countess of —— does not so much as invite him to dinner, without pre-assuring herself by a mysterious missive whom he will he best pleased to meet at her table; whether it suit his will and pleasure to take out the young Marchioness of A——, and whether he have any objection to her including in her invitations the young and promising Member for Pushinfield! The poor man is not allowed to stir a step, or eat a cutlet, but there are decoys and pitfalls in ambush around him. Against these, one of his surest defences is his Private Secretary.

One day, having an idle hour on our hands, somewhat nearer noon than it is our custom to be met with on the pavé, we took Thomas Grosvenor, Esq. by surprise by an early visit, and were not a little amused to find him busy with scissors and paste; *not* making pincushions for a charity bazaar for New Zealand missionaries, but evidently caught in the toils of authorship. Instantly thrusting his paraphernalia into a drawer, with a most unsecretary-like blush, he denied the hard impeachment. But with one bird's eye view, the state of the case had been discovered. Even then we knew somewhat of the mechanism of book-making, and were satisfied that the manufactory had gained a supernumerary workman.

Luckily for Tom he was enabled to set at nought our officious cross-questioning, by the arrival of the heads of a country church-building deputation; who came to settle their hour of audience, and send up, in presence of the Secretary, such a pilot-balloon as might fore-arm and forewarn his parton of the object of their mission. For it is seldom the policy of deputations to take the head of a department by surprise. It sounds better in the country to have had their answer delivered to them in good round periods. A crabbed sentence or two, interlarded with ministerial interjections, constitutes a slight thrown upon themselves and their mission.

After remaining an auditor of this gratuitous interview just long enough to admire the skill with which Grosvenor contrived to enhance the ministerial dignity by consulting his note-book as to hours and audience, (incidentally citing between his teeth appointments with the Chancellor and the Archbishop of Canterbury, princes of the blood and presidents of academies,) and the still greater art with which by a word or two thrown out on the question of the objects of the deputation, he gave them to understand that, in the audience they solicited, it would be unanswerably demonstrated to them that two and two make five,—we thought it decent to withdraw.

A short time afterwards, the town rang with the merits of a new political pamphlet on a popular question, which was pretty generally attributed to the noble ministerial patron of Thomas Grosvenor. The clubs and coteries pronounced it to be an able and luminous performance. The dinner-tables of the West-end went into paroxysms of applause;—for a week, even the entrechats of the favourite danseuse were overlooked.

The reviews, indeed, particularly those opposed to the policy of the government, ventured to discover, like Tilleyrand of his friend's maiden speech, that it contained many good and new things; but that the good things were not new, or the new things good. They even presumed to point out the origin of its statistics in certain obscure pamphlets—the origin of its ethics in certain visitation sermons—the origin of its arguments in the parliamentary debates of a preceding session. That these were skilfully put together, they did not deny—*too* skilfully they apprehended for the inexperienced and aristocratic hand of the noble head of the —— department. In short, they insisted upon it that some "influence behind the throne" (or desk) had presided over the concoction.

The next time we called upon Tom Grosvenor, (on second thoughts, upon this occasion he saw fit for the first time to return our numerous visits, and call upon ourself) he avowed himself indignant at the disparaging view taken by the public of the capacity of his noble patron. He assured us, and hinted a wish we would assure others, that his lordship was a man generally underrated,—a man who had distinguished himself at college, and would have equally distinguished himself in Parliament, had not the malice of the fates placed him in precisely that one of the two Houses where his peculiar line of abilities was comparatively unavailable. In short, every word uttered by the devoted Private Secretary tended to prove that his lordship was the only man in England capable of the authorship of the capital pamphlet of which six thousand had been really sold, and to the last edition of which, "fifteen thousand" was prefixed by way of advertisement.

It was no business of ours. Whether his lordship wrote the pamphlet, or the leading articles that praised it, or the advertisements that puffed, was to us a matter of complete indifference. Nevertheless, since the Private Secretary of an author cannot be supposed to be equally susceptible concerning the merits of a work as the author *in propriâ personâ*, we took occasion, seeing that Tom was in so communicative a vein, to discuss the subject-matter of the pamphlet—to differ from its political views, and play upon its literary pretensions.

Then, indeed, had we occasion to admire the blind and devoted adherency of the Secretary! A high-pressure engine could scarcely have burst with a more alarming explosion. He "begged leave to differ from us entirely;" which means that he differed from us *toto cœlo* without leave given or taken. From the sucking-dove eloquence of Private Secretaryship, he suddenly thundered into a Boanerges!

As we said before, we cared very little either for the pamphlet or its authorship; and when Grosvenor quitted the room, contented ourself with self-gratulation that his morning visits were septennial concessions. We could not, however, help recalling to mind the self-command and gentleness of speech with which we had formerly seen him dismiss the intrusions of certain poor relations of his own into his office at the Treasury, (who came to sponge upon him for government stationery,) compared with this vehement outbreak. He appeared to have gained wonderfully in lungs, and fearfully in temper, since his transformation into a Secretary.

Six months afterwards, the Gazette announced his promotion to a colonial appointment of weight and responsibility; and for many following weeks, government paragraphs prated of his audiences with the Colonial Secretary, and the despatch with which a government steamer had been put in preparation for his departure for his seat of government. On his presentation to kiss hands and take leave of the august face of majesty, he underwent knighthood; and lo! the name of "Sir Thomas Grosvenor" became inscribed in the category of public men, upon whose comings and goings it is the delight of the newspapers to expatiate.

From that period, I heard nothing of His Excellency, save when, every couple of months or so, the "organs of government" announced that despatches had been received from him at the Colonial Office; and once, when a florid article in the Quarterly Review, anent the state and prospects of the obscure island submitted to his legislation, adverted incidentally to the wondrous improvements to which his brief legislation had given rise; in prose closely akin in style and diction to the renowned pamphlet concerning which we had presumed to differ from the incipient knight.

Prosperity seemed to have laid him asleep. He was like a gorged boa constrictor. We felt assured that, in ten years' time, Sir Thomas would come back with a liver complaint and claims to a pension,—marry the daughter of some Scottish Earl,—get into Parliament and the Canton; and subside into a pursy, prosy, middle-aged gentleman; converting, perhaps, his knighthood into a baronetcy in the crush of some coronation batch.

But ministries, like captains, are casual things; and it fell out that the patron of Sir Thomas and his colleagues, were among the breakages of the day;—swept from the surface of, official life by one of the whirl winds that occasionally arise in even the best regulated kingdoms.

Other patrons emitted prose and preferment in their place—which knew them no longer; and in the course of the session following their downfall, among their protégés chosen out to become marks for parliamentary pecking, in proof of the corruption and incompetency of their administration, was the luckless Sir Thomas Grosvenor!—A crack speech, got up for the especial purpose, pointed out his seat of government as the head-quarters of jobbery and abuse. The absent are always in the wrong—the feeble have no friends unluckily, the Ex-secretary had a few, of the kind which wise men pray to be delivered from!—His former patron took up his cudgels precisely in the style to bring down upon both the severest retaliation. Sir Thomas Grosvenor was recalled. Sir Thomas Grosvenor had to answer for himself in pamphlets and petitions—too happy to escape the bar of the House. It was in vain he appealed to the party whose patronage had hatched him into existence. Of that existence, they affected to be scarcely cognizant. "Who was this Sir Thomas Grosvenor? Oh yes! they recollected. Formerly Private Secretary to their friend the Marquis; a useful young man enough, whose services government had liberally rewarded. Pity that he should have been placed in a situation to which his abilities and experience were unequal!—Sir Thomas Grosvenor had committed their party—and of Sir Thomas Grosvenor, consequently, for his sake and their own, for the future, the less said the better."

"From the party quoad party I could have borne all this!" observed my old schoolfellow, when, with a shaking hand and jaundiced complexion, he sat beside me, telling me his doleful story. "But that man, whom I so diligently served, and who swore he would peril soul and body to serve me in return,—that man, whose official blunders I screened—whose speeches I made—whose pamphlet I wrote!—Little, very little, does the world conjecture the severe labour and dirty work that enters into the duties of a PRIVATE SECRETARY."

End Of Volume One